"Herein lies an intertwining of family trees and family stories that is a trail of skeletons, transgressions, lies and betrayals bearing many of the consequences William Henry created in his life. The truth lies in his DNA (deoxyribonucleic acid) a molecule that carries the genetic instructions which will forever change the lives of the many whose paths he has crossed.

I had a great time reading this book, it was an adventure."

(Ms. Sam Giordano – Vice President, Programs - Clark County Nevada Genealogical Society.)

⚒⚒

"Joyce delivers a powerful story of knowing, accepting and then acting on betrayal. We learn how each new generation carries the problems of the previous one and how each person has to find his or her individual way to deal with the life they are born into. Quotations at the beginning of each chapter help to capture the sometimes harsh truths of life. The DNA information strengthen Joyce's work, giving us even more perspective. This is a must read for anyone seeking understanding and answers to --- WHY?"

(Cynthia L. De Boer – Inspirational Speaker - Author - Prosthetic Eye Advocate – www.memyselfandeyebook.com)

⚒⚒

"Generations Intertwine," is more proof of the power of Joyces' writing. She doesn't just throw words at a page and hope they stick, she's sharp and clear. She knows what she's talking about."

(Nick Adams, Author – University of Southern Mississippi, Hattiesburg, Mississippi)

GENERATIONS INTERTWINE

The Rest of the Story

Joyce K. Gatschenberger

ISBN: 0999193902
ISBN 13: 9780999193907
Library of Congress Control Number: 2017911742
Joyce, Henderson, NV

Dedicated to
Brian, Tarena, Erica, Kiyah and Van

CONTENTS

FORWARD

*"There is no greater agony than bearing
an untold story inside you."*

Maya Angelou

*"When someone shows you who they are,
believe them the first time."*

Maya Angelou

*"The need for change bulldozed a road
down the center of my mind."*

Maya Angelou

CHAPTER 1
LEAVING IN STAGES

*"There are always women who will take
men on their own terms. If I were a man,
I wouldn't bother to change while there
are women like that around."*

Ann Oakley

Courage, a precious commodity intertwined with betrayal, imprints early on the Henry family. An unexpected attack, which triggers the commodity, initiates from
within their lineage, banding them together to withstand
the onslaught.

William leaves his family in stages. His deceit and betrayal are unexpected and complete. Secrets abound behind his departure, causing wasted emotional and physical
energy. He is not as adept as the nocturnal slug, however,

at evasion and illusion. Although these traits are naturally occurring for both species, the elusive bug has mastered the technique.

Lack of personal courage and William's desire to begin life anew could spare his family intense pain, but he chose not to take that road – his road is easier for him, yet harder for those who love him. Remembering their lives together, and reflecting on interactive conversations, Kaye, his wife of thirty-five years, fails to detect subtle signs of William's stages of separation.

≕+ +≔

Military life offers overwhelming opportunities for Chief Master Sergeant William Henry of the elite Search and Rescue Squad and is a bastion of extended periods for living as a single person without worries or burdens of married life. Tours in overseas locations and intermittent assignments on stateside military bases offer exciting options for him to locate vulnerable partners with which to establish relationships. The Mockingbird, William's kindred spirit, keenly watches and takes lessons, thus learning to deposit offspring into prepared nests and then ignoring the nurturing process. Such situations affect the Henry family for generations.

William is in his full glory when receiving military transfer orders. He operates on a "cycle." When the demands and concerns of life elevate military orders, either short-term within the United States or long-term overseas – save the day. Thus leaving unresolved issues incomplete and undiscussed.

William's lifestyle operates on daily reoccurring adrenaline rushes. Unfortunately, this erratic schedule extends far beyond his military life and disrupts the household routine. Kaye suggests that his behavior is inappropriate. He scoffs and states that "he and the guys" are just letting off some steam. After unrequited requests for the rowdy guests to leave their home, the children settle into bed, and Kaye reluctantly retires. The rousing clamor from the party, wharfing from the front of the house, rushes down the hallway and blasts against the bedroom doors. Unfortunately, Kaye now becomes the loud-mouthed, nagging wife, begrudging her husband a few hours of "letting off steam with the boys."

Kaye hears rumors from the returning military detachment of "extracurricular" activities concerning William, but when questioned, he swears true faithfulness to their marriage. What a great set-up for him – live with the wife, kiss the kids, and have fun too!

Slowly, and inconspicuously to Kaye, like the daily rotation of the earth, William's separation begins. Deployments more frequent and calls less frequent. The report of incidences during deployment increase and come to a high point when he returns from a lengthy military tour to Germany. Exiting the aircraft, Kaye notes a splint on William's right index finger. He struggles to carry his duffle bag and military equipment. Kaye, meeting the transport, notes that the other search and rescue personnel offer no help to William as he is exiting the plane and they eye him, suspiciously.

Approaching the tarmac, Kaye notes the presence of a large bandage extending from the tip of William's finger down to his wrist, secured with a pressure dressing.

Something, possibly emotionally charged, occurred between the troops during this deployment. Kaye senses that it involves William and the airmen in his group. When questioned, William explains that while examining his new pocketknife, it slips and cuts a deep slice in his right finger. This incident almost delays his departure from Germany because he is in the hospital emergency room. He spends the next few weeks on light military duty with frequent visits to the medical clinic. Kaye's suspicion meter should have activated.

⇥ ⇤

For the next three decades, William's commitment to their union degrades. Constantly searching, he is restless and unsettled. Lacking the personal courage to approach Kaye honestly, William slowly withdraws from their relationship.

Another negative thread weaves throughout their marriage – the adverse influence of the in-laws on their family. The influence of William's mother and sisters is harmful. Their efforts to undermine and separate William from the union is an ever-present undertone. Managing this situation forces William to create two separate personas.

When William and Kaye spend time away from his parents and can interact with their children, William tempers his wonder lust with admiration and love for his family. However, during visits to his parent's home, William engages in conversations that are verbally degrading to Kaye. His mother takes special delight in these exchanges. This flip-flop stance is confusing for Kaye. Showing his birth family that his spouse is unworthy, continues to usher in his separation from the marriage. This bipolar activity gains his mother's sympathy since he carries the heavy burden of an unsatisfying marriage partner.

However, these family conversations do not extend to discussions involving the children. Grandma delights in having grandchildren. If the marriage is to dissolve, she will help her son gain custody of her lineage. The foundation for child custody begins early in the marriage and grandma is going to be on the winning side. Kaye is naïve to the back-story workings of evil. Believing that honesty, love, and sharing are the basis of marriage, is her downfall. Little does Kaye realize that when a dishonest person is uncomfortable with their situation, they simply remove themselves, either physically or emotionally? Honesty and courage are orphan ideas.

William's life changes following his military discharge. Having spent twenty-two years in a Crusader system provides opportunities in the form of military deployments and small tour assignments. Now, as a civilian without the determined, regulated routine of military life, William loses his direction. Taking orders and following routines became part of William. He is dependent on that regimented style to guide him in everyday life since it provides escape avenues when his wonder lust becomes his prominent guiding force. Military discharge and civilian integration in Nevada begins a most difficult mission – a self-monitoring lifestyle.

Now, he is at loose ends civilian life challenges him. Once a person embraces an identity that defines their sense of self, they also embrace certain traits of that identity; i.e. shyness, irritability, deception, lying, and laziness. Over time, when a person expresses these traits long enough, they assume that these particular traits are part of their DNA characteristics and therefore, unchangeable. William is quite comfortable working within this described outline and designs his life around the familiar pattern. In other words, in the military, he could play the part of a loving family man and still enjoy the alluring life as a single person. However, now as a civilian, he needs to recreate that same type of lifestyle and decide how to continue the double fraud – married man, single man. William strikes that balance by finding an out-of-town job, yet continues living as a husband and father. This arrangement is fragile, at best, and it is destined to be the chink in his armor.

Kaye's employment as a registered nurse throughout their marriage adds income to the family transition needs. Her income now exceeds William's retirement supplement; this increases his disconnection. Again, refusing to discuss his feelings, he assumes an irritated, unsettled attitude and posture. This estranged environment begins William's search for a series of intermittent jobs. His resume' contains duties at a local news station, maintenance person for a day care center and sales person for snow cones. William soon falls into a cycle of chronic depression that showed only hints of itself early in the marriage. Its' spiral comes faster and wider as time progresses. He is surly and angry. The marital relationship suffers greatly.

Kaye notices that William spends extended time away from home with less accounting for his schedule. He secures a full-time position at Hoover Dam in Las Vegas, NV.

During this period, he begins an illicit affair with a woman in the visitor's center office. The affair is exposed when he and Kaye attend the annual company Christmas party.

Entering the party, William immediately leaves Kaye's side and rushes to a woman sitting with her husband in the kitchen of the host's home. William nudges between the couple and begins nuzzling the woman's neck while talking in muffled, pleading romantic tones. The woman initially welcomes the advance by leaning into it, but stiffened her posture when she notes Kaye's appearance. Kaye has followed William into the room since he makes such a quick search upon their arrival.

Kaye's suspicion meter is flashing brightly again and quickly registers. Even with Kaye's presence, William is reluctant to release his physical entanglement. Only after the woman insists that it may be inappropriate for such an obvious show of affection, does William relent his advance. He backs away, saunters past Kaye and walks back into the front room without response. The guests observing this encounter hold silent, watching. After eyeing "the woman," Kaye breaks eye contact, turns and leaves the kitchen. Much like witnesses to a gruesome accident who refuse to offer details knowing that their actions will surely convict the suspect, the guests freeze in place.

Unable to respond appropriately, Kaye rushes to the billowing comfort of an overstuffed recliner in the front room – William turns and slyly escapes to the front porch.

Blinded by love for this man without reserve, she can hardly admit her shock and denial – to acknowledge he is having an amorous affair with another woman will crush her belief in their solid marriage. However, after examining similar situations, she begins to realize the cycle. William spends a tremendous amount of time hiding his marital infidelities. Deciding to reveal this extramarital affair on this particular night, with this particular woman, has occupied William's mind for a few days before the Christmas party. What possesses a man to betray his marriage vows?

Well, after careful consideration, Kaye concludes that men do it, and sometimes women, because they can, and it is that simple and that complicated. If a man is going to cheat, he cheats. Simple and true. The grave aspect, which unfaithful partners do not consider or do not care about, is the path of torrid destruction that it plows through the family unit and the loving hearts of the children. It is a shameful and sorrowful thing.

Kaye has given her heart and soul to a man who is unfaithful. Horrifying as it is, Kaye and William do not discuss this incident as they drive home from the Christmas party. What is wrong with her? Is she an idiot? Is she in shock? Does she sense that the discussion will destroy their marriage? Kaye knows the answers to all of these questions. William has already destroyed the base of trust between them. She imagines that William set up this scene as a test for her. If he can pull off this obvious public show of affection for another woman in her presence, then he will be successful in other whoring pursuits. Unfortunately, he knows Kaye too well!

⇥ ⇤

The final stage of William's leaving became evident at a most reprehensible time - he dies. Following his burial, an exam of his paperwork reveals the completion of his departure. A few years before his death, around the turn of the new millennium, William accepts a job working for an insurance company in Colorado. His friend, Mr. Menendez, manages this company. William's position is one of insurance assessment and evaluation for homes damaged by natural disasters. He travels out-of-town for job orientation. However, as the month's pass, William's return trips home became fewer. Phone calls to home and family members became infrequent. He did have a cell phone.

When Kaye suggests that she come to spend the weekend, the reasons for avoidance begin:

"I share a tiny apartment with a lot of guys. There's no room." On the other hand, "I'm in a bad room and don't know how long I will be here," he states with conviction.

He also relates that his car is not dependable. When he can make more money, he can buy a better vehicle and travel back home more often. Again, Kaye's suspicion meter is blinking! There is no proof.

This verbal battering continues until William stops returning home and does not answer his phone, at least will not answer Kaye's calls. She knows something is wrong. William, as usual, is hiding something. Like a squirrel hiding nuts for the winter frost. A few months pass, and after repeated unanswered calls, Kaye is planning an unannounced visit to Colorado. She books the plane ticket, dreading what she may find.

※⁺ ⁺※

Kaye is running late for work this particular morning, and she grabs her keys without much thought except that if she did not drive a little too fast down the road, she would be late. Feeling disoriented, she automatically opens the back door and runs smack into William, standing on the back porch steps.

Emotions flood and overwhelm her body and psyche. Kaye feels weak as the color drains from her face and is sure that she resembles a male Japanese stage actor impersonating a female role. Multitudes of questions crumple up in her brain as so much waded up notebook paper and block any logical thought. The breath leaves her body, and sanity leaves the realm of reason. Her hands fly up into the air resembling the stance of a dedicated ballerina while all her bundles, including car keys, clamor down in disarray onto the porch. The deafening sound surely matches the clamor of home invaders rummaging through dresser drawers in search of family jewels. Within an instant, her field of vision hones in on her son, Benedict, standing sheepishly behind her husband. Words fail her!

The trio stands motionless on the porch, expressionless, locked in a gaze that screams a thousand questions, yet says nothing. William breaks the standoff.

"Well, guess I surprised you, didn't I?" A faint, sick, sly smile veils over his face increasing the glint in his eyes. "I flew in on the red-eye and wanted to get here early."

Fumbling for words, Kaye utters, "I wish that you would have called, I could take the day off. I am late for work, and it is a busy day at the clinic. The other nurse called in sick, and the docs have a lot of surgery scheduled," she manages to fragment a reply while fumbling with keys and moving toward the car.

William and Benedict stand motionless, side-by-side on the back porch steps watching as Kaye backs out of the driveway. Looking much like a pair of trained hunting dogs who just lost their prized catch of the season – the pup excitedly waiting to "tree-the-catch" with the older tested bloodhound, bound to the rules of the hunt."

While watching his mother's car disappear down the road, Benedict says with a sense of the obvious, "Well, Dad, I guess that you surely put one over on mom this time. She didn't expect to see either one of us this morning."

"Yeah, Son, I pulled it off this time. Well, let's go in the house and get some coffee. I'm sure that your mom has a well-stocked kitchen," William says with a hint of sly confidence as though he has just pulled off a successful jewel heist.

Questions whirl through Kaye's head. What makes William come home at this time? Why is their son, Benedict, with him? How does Benedict know of his visit? Does William avoid calling so that he can catch her off guard, or did he want to surprise her? Does he arrive at the house just as she is leaving for work to avoid the question? Thoughts bounce as though they are shooting microwave charges inside her brain clouding her consciousness. There is no time to concentrate on relationship issues because, by the time she arrives in the parking lot, the clinic is already buzzing with surgery activity and patient concerns. The nurse practitioner meets Kaye at the employee entrance with an uncharacteristically, irritated voice,

"We are waiting for you. Today is one of those busy days, and it looks like it will only get worse." Kaye needs to be at her best.

CHAPTER 2
THE REAL REASON

"If we don't change directions soon,
we'll end up where we're going."

Professor Irwin Corey

K aye is embroiled in the hectic spin of the clinic when the front office secretary notifies her of a telephone call. Taking the call at the nurse's station, she hears an unexpected, yet familiar voice, her husband, William, requesting a doctor appointment,

"Just for a check-up, nothing serious," with curiosity in his voice.

He is reluctant to offer additional information. He just wants to know if Kaye can arrange the appointment for later that day. It takes her a moment to understand the situation – William came home for a medical reason, not to see her. He must be scared of something, something he could not fix or avoid or demean.

William keeps his doctor appointment later that day at the VA (Veteran's Administration) clinic, completes his blood work and stops by the nurses' station as he leaves. All afternoon Kaye wonders – what scares William? Why did he return home unannounced and go directly to the medical clinic for a check-up? Kaye senses that she will never know the whole, true story of this issue either.

Kaye yearns to learn the reason for his homecoming. William was elusive as a bird hiding prized material for the spring nest. Their conversation merry-go-rounds in a superficial nature, focusing on medical check-ups to stay healthy and well. It is obvious that William did not come home to see his family. He discovered something in his body that scares him, and it brought him to his knees, figuratively. He needs to determine the cause. At his urging, Kaye calls as soon as the blood work results came from the lab. He shows her the paperwork indicating his return appointment.

The next few days, their home fills with tension and an uneasy quiet – Kaye asks questions which William does not answer. The mood changes markedly with an evening phone call from the VA doctor. William lifts the receiver, seems to listen, and yet stares blankly into space. Hanging up the receiver, he stares unemotionally into space saying,

"I have a doctor appointment tomorrow," his words trail off into silence.

Within the next two weeks, William and Kaye are visiting another clinic in Las Vegas, Nevada. The medical provider evaluates a large nodule located in William's left groin area. As Kaye learns, by accompanying him to these appointments, William notices a golf-ball sized nodule and thought it was a lower abdominal hernia. However, evaluation confirms a soft tissue sarcoma. Cancer is a medical condition listed under "presumptive causes" from his military exposure to Agent Orange, a cancer-causing defoliant. A medical workup verifies the diagnosis at the Air Force Base Hospital and the Veteran's Administration. The medical decision is to perform a surgical excision of the tumor and hope to secure a clean border of the tumor, thereby, decreasing the chances of the tumor re-occurring.

A series of chemotherapy infusions follow in an attempt to kill any remaining cancer cells. A civilian oncologist and cancer surgeon perform their duties well, and the V.A. exhausts all their medical interventions. However, blood tests confirm a spreading of his sarcoma. After careful consideration and research of available resources, William and Kaye get a second opinion from a trusted cancer treatment center – M.D. Anderson Center in Houston, Texas.

This treatment routine is not covered under the V.A. system but is sanctioned by Kaye's employee medical insurance program. Meaning that she needs to remain a V.A. employee – a huge challenge. Kaye depleted her sick and vacation leave balances when she accompanied William to his medical appointments. The human resources department advises her of an employee-sharing plan in which her colleagues would donate some of their vacation time for use for this situation. Kaye can accompany William to M.D. Anderson and console him when the practitioners give him the same diagnosis and prognosis that his local doctors presented.

William becomes even more combative and secretive. "I want you docs to show me exactly where those tumors are. Where exactly in my body is all of this cancer stuff. If I am going to die or have this poison put into my arm, I want to see where this damn fuss is. You people are all just trying to gyp me, get my money so that you can buy more drugs, and make me sicker. I will not die no matter what you do to me. You are all just quacks. None of you knows anything. It's all just a bunch or hogwash."

His behavior is that of an angry, belligerent recluse. His object of mistreatment is, of course, the person who cares for him and loves him the most – Kaye. Her husband's rants and raves are often and vicious. "I told you to get your filthy hands off of that wheelchair. I can roll those wheels myself. You act like I am an invalid."

His health is deteriorating, he will not be returning to his job in Colorado, and he acts as though he is struggling to keep a secret that is very difficult to keep. It becomes obvious to Kaye that William intends to come home to Nevada, get treatment from his doctor for "a hernia" and then return to his out-of-state job. This routine is quickly disappearing along with William's persona.

William becomes creatively devious and angry when his options are slim. He does not like accepting others' ideas. He secretively calls his sister and arranges another futile trip to M.D. Anderson Medical Center. Ignoring pleadings, they go, they receive the same prognosis, and they return home.

It soon becomes obvious to William's work colleagues that he will not be returning to his job in Colorado. His boss, Mr. Menendez, makes an unannounced visit from

Colorado to William's hospital room one dreary afternoon. He wants to assess the situation for himself. It is obvious from the appearance of William's ashen skin and sullen appearance, that what he hears on the telephone from William and the truth of his medical reality are two very different situations – realization spreads over Mr. Menendez's disillusioned face. It is as if he owns a car lot and is losing his top-selling salesperson. Kaye notices his confused facial expression and motions him to step away from William's bedside and speak with her.

"What is wrong with William? I thought that he was going to have a simple surgery and then get back to work, I never expected anything like this." Mr. Menendez, speaking with a quiver in his voice, raises his hands to cup his face.

Mrs. Menendez stands close with an expectant expression on her face echoing her husband's sentiment, "Yes, we just talked with him, and he said that he is doing well."

Speaking in a hushed tone, Kaye attempts to explain to the couple that William is dying of cancer and obviously will not be returning to either Colorado or his job. "William is dying. He did not do well with chemotherapy, and his body is very weak. I know him well, and he is angry about something. Do you know of anything that might be troubling him? Is there something that he is trying to keep secret? He gets agitated when he is thinking about something but doesn't want to talk about it." Kaye looks expectantly into the eyes of a man who appears to be kind and is concerned for her husband's welfare, searching for an answer.

Hearing this, the two visitors hesitate in their conversation, acting as though they have a multitude of questions that now may go unanswered, much like a raven who forages a shiny piece yet keeps secret the hiding place. The disillusioned couple talk in hushed tones and then whisper their "good-byes" as they slowly leave the room. Mr. Menendez hesitates at the door, turning slowly to look back as though he has the final remark. Just as he is about to speak, his wife nudges his arm and motions for him to continue their exit. Kaye senses that the bigger story is indeed in Colorado, but pieces will unfold in Nevada. Little does she know how very right her senses are?

The emotionally rattled couple, ready for their Colorado return, state, "We need to get back and arrange things with our business. We are so sad that William will not be returning to Colorado. Everyone will surely miss him. He has a lot of personal ties in the area."

They turn briefly toward William's bedside, bend down to softly touch his cheek and mumble a few incoherent statements in his ear. The response is immediate and expressive throughout William's body. His posture stiffens, and his breath inhales much like an oak tree bulwarked against an approaching hurricane. However, William remains verbally silent, like a fire engine refusing to answer the beckoning blare of the fire bell.

Kaye is certain that the couple possesses the rest of her husband's elusive story, but will never confess. There exists an unhealthy alliance between this triad. William has already convinced himself that whatever the truth is in Colorado, it will not be a truth in Nevada.

Well, William never makes it back to his life in Colorado. A sneaking suspicion arises and takes hold that his secret life in Colorado entangles a plethora of unanswered questions. He is caught and cannot return home to answer them, leaving unfinished business.   Kaye's haunting suspicions linger in the air, like a threatening thunderstorm. The story that William began in Colorado would be unfolding in a most unlikely manner for her family, through future generations.

CHAPTER 3
LEFT BEHIND

"Old books that have ceased to be of service should no more be abandoned than should old friends who have ceased to give pleasure."

Bernard Baruch

William's resting place is Camp Bender military cemetery in Illinois, the state of his birth. His thirty-five-year marriage obviously a farce - a fact soon to be revealed. William's children, two daughters, and a son, truly mourn his passing. They will not tolerate any word against his memory. Their eyes reflect a father who is the best at everything, including being a dad. They are his legacy, his prodigy, and yet, do not understand him. His grand-daughter, Dove-Whispering, however, holds the secret to the family history. She can ask the most probing questions and develop the path that will reveal the truth, whether it be in genealogy or relationships. This ability proves to be both the heartache and redeeming quality of her family unit. Unanswered questions and shadowy people disappear when faced with an illuminating and inquisitive mind.

⚡ ⚡

The Henry family legacy begins by investigating William's life, and that means reviewing the paperwork left behind. The briefcase, which holds his work, is the last bastion to examine and is located in the corner of William's office.

Searching through the folders reveals forms related to the insurance recovery business for which William worked. Kaye assembles them and makes a mental note to send them to William's boss in Colorado, Mr. Menendez. Further investigation reveals an assortment of paperwork relating to everyday life, i.e. sales receipts, company water bills, a bill for a tire change, a receipt for groceries. Kaye has almost resigns herself to the fact that no further secrets remain as she looks through the discarded paperwork until she notes the last, back pocket of the briefcase. Her search reveals a collection of papers and known, yet unfamiliar, sexual items.

A chilling sense grips her, if she continues to reach into the pocket, her life could forever change, so she hesitates. Suspicion and curiosity overcame her like the unstoppable contractions of childbirth, and this urge commands attention. Her fingers trace and caress the collection of papers until she feels a slightly crinkled document announcing its presence by individuality. Pulling the inviting pliable form from seclusion, she notes a lightly scented parchment that feels sensual and intriguing. The accompanying sexual items, intentionally nestled alongside, are strangely alluring. This discovery reveals William's other life, the hidden one! Instinctively, Kaye knows that finding this information will challenge her naivety and shatter her children's lives as well, so she hesitates, again. Ever so slowly she lifts the carnal parchment from its hiding place.

William lovingly wrote the sensual note to his sweetheart. After 35 years, Kaye knows his handwriting intimately. The collection of sexual toys positioned next to the letter is obviously part of his relationship with his love partner in Colorado. Apparently, William plans to return to his mistress after his little medical check-up in Nevada, but he is caught and he cannot return. Possibly, William is planning to have his health needs resolved and then travel back to his little love nest to continue his hidden double life for as long as it will last. The unanswered and undiscussed issues.

Another small, inconspicuous white note in the bottom of the briefcase almost goes unnoticed. Examining it reveals a bank deposit from an account in William's name. Kaye's link to his other life is the "800" phone number listed on this note. She calls. The bank statement being sent to William's sister in another state is not a document she can access. However, Kaye manages to secure the contents of the account attached to the statement and decides to distribute the funds to their children. Distributing the money means that she must reveal the source of the funds.

The oldest daughter, Michelle, and youngest child, Anne, are equally devastated. Their dad is a knight-in-shining-armor. They grow up believing that he would do anything to protect them from all of the bad things in life. He is the one that they go to when they need protection. When their car needs repair, they call Dad. He is an imaginary savior figure or an example of the type of man a woman may want to marry and live happily-ever-after-with. Michelle craves the aura of excitement and intensity that her father portrays. He will often party and keep the home environment busy and complicated. Anne, the more sedate and sensitive daughter, envisions that her father will guide and counsel her when life became too big to handle. Her father offers the joke for her when she needs to laugh and is always willing to make a balloon animal on a rainy afternoon to brighten her spirits.

Presenting their daughters with funds from the account means so much more than just money. It represents a familial betrayal down to their deep, inner core. It means that the foundation of their relationship with their father is a lie. They struggle to realize that their childhood developed with a father who is deceitful and secretive and is one who cannot be trusted. It makes them doubt the very value system they rely on to determine their place in the world. A universe, created by someone who no longer exists, destroyed. Those memories are now shaded and doubtful. Kaye knows that from this moment on, each will have a difficult time forming a loving, caring, and long-term relationship with a man that they cannot trust.

Relationships between fathers and sons can be complicated. Benedict, their son, and oldest child is a quiet, stoic man who experiences a convoluted affiliation with his father. William is his scouting leader, helping him to attain the level of Eagle Scout. Benedict learns to drive a car and shoot a gun under William's guidance. However, William does not teach Benedict to channel his emotions positively or to show respect for his mother.

When Kaye presents the funds to Benedict that gloomy, dreadful afternoon, he yells at her as though she is a common street whore, spitting words at her formed in the dark, sleazy Bourbon streets of New Orleans. He is in total denial and disbelief. Kaye knows that he can be violent when he is angry, and she fears that if he does not find a constructive outlet for the hurt and pain he is obviously experiencing, he will internalize the feelings and destroy all that is still good and kind within himself. Her anguish for her son is indescribable.

Benedict continues to maintain a stoic, intense persona and finds it difficult to integrate into an adult relationship with Kaye since he irrationally blames her for the deceit within the marriage. Avoiding crowds and public areas helps him withdraw from functions and society in general. He would rather spend his resources on computer endeavors. This, Kaye believes, is a direct result of his loss of trust and belief in his father. The betrayal of his father is complete and lifelong. Kaye's aching heart cannot repair or love away this reality. The only person who seems to warm his heart is his niece, Dove-Whispering – Michelle's daughter. She knows the special part of his heart that he keeps safe and protected just for her. Dove-Whispering warms his heart as no one else can. The passage of time will prove if the value of trust and love will endure for Benedict.

The light morning mist hangs heavy in the sky as Michelle struggles to lift the heavy cardboard box into the trunk of her well-worn vehicle. The container is marked with various words such as kitchen, fragile, bathroom, etc. since it has been her companion through many relocations. She wants to get an early start on her drive since the hot desert sun could be blistery by high noon, and the black heated tarmac would occupy the first part of their trip. This move will be a new start in her teaching career and for her teen-aged daughter, Dove-Whispering, as well. Michelle hoped to find tenure and appreciation within the Green County school district through her classroom dedication and work as a science director, but the politics of teaching always got there first. Questionable forces within the Green County school district, which were set in force long before she arrived, destined her departure.

Eight a.m. chimes on her cell phone as she passes her sleepy, teenage daughter. Dove-Whispering comes half-hopping down the stairs carrying an assortment of bedroom blankets, and doggy treats wrapped haphazardly into the old laundry basket. It seems to Michelle that her daughter is always in perpetual motion, but maybe it is that Michelle is finding it more challenging to maintain her own youthful, fluid movements. Whatever it is, she finds it more challenging each time she and her daughter decide to change their place of residence. Michelle is a military brat, moved many times in her younger years and is very familiar with the finer points of packing, storing, and repacking, but she is getting a little weary of it in her adult life.

She watches Dove-Whispering and notices that her daughter's long, straight, black hair blowing wildly in the crisp morning wind resembles the shiny pompoms that Michelle used as a cheerleading mascot in her youth. Dove-Whispering's teenage body is agile and flexible. Just watching her reminds Michelle of her younger days. Sometimes, Michelle wonders if her daughter knows how strikingly beautiful she is and if she values that part of her legacy that is Native American. Dove-Whispering's dark brown, intense eyes often seclude her intense inner thoughts. The intensity of those thoughts often occupies Dove-Whispering's self-talk language that she narrates in her head to sort out the complex issues of her world. Never the less, her genetic mixture of German and American Indian heritage produced a most beautiful child who is pensive and watchful. She is born in the new millennium, and her bright future is as sure as the promising new decade.

Dove-Whispering is all too familiar with the moving process and knows what to pack so that items can be reached easily upon arriving. Michelle and Dove-Whispering load most of the smaller household items and kitchen utensils since they spent the past few weeks gathering boxes and using the old plastic tubs stored in the back bedroom closet for just such an occasion. Michelle knows how to pack her car so that she will have enough room to see through the back window during their cross-country drive to Colorado.

Benedict, her older brother, assures her that he will be at her apartment early in the morning to help load the heavy furniture, but still, Michelle anxiously awaits. Her brother initially was against her move from Nevada since she would be moving away from him and their younger sister, Anne. He is also cautious about her relocation since she would not have anyone in Colorado to watch out for her protection. Benedict hopes that Dove-Whispering's father would have more of a presence in his niece's life, but that is not the case. Dove-Whispering's father, a man of American Indian heritage, chose not to be active in his daughter's early life and now that she is in her teen years, there was a yearning within Dove-Whispering which no one else seems able to fill. As though a faraway voice keeps calling her to search for something hidden just out of reach, yet she would never be able to find. Much like the echo of a repeating saga, that haunts the dreamer. This unanswered call left a void in Dove-Whispering's personal life that resembles a widening cavern. Benedict could see that his niece was blossoming into an inquisitive, precocious teen-aged girl and he knows that Dove-Whispering has an inner restlessness that was just now stirring within her. He was always comfortable calling her by her given Christian name, Dove-Whispering, but he wonders if she will want her new friends to know her simply as "Dove." Sometimes, a new location requires a new personality and a new past. His favorite and only niece is certainly capable of inventing whatever life she intends to live. However, as the moving date approached, he could see his sister, Michelle's commitment. Benedict is determined to help make their move easier. He also wants to make this morning of the move a little less hectic if he can.

Michelle can see the apartment manager walking across the parking lot toward her to do the final inspection and she would be irritated if the apartment was not clean and empty. Michelle and the manager maintain a friendly relationship, but a few testy interactions occurred during their two-year lease. The tenant-exit needs to go smoothly, and

Michelle needs the money from her security deposit to pay for gas for the car trip.

The apartment manager can see that the apartment isn't empty as she approaches and says with a sly tone,

"Well, looks like we are running behind schedule this morning, Michelle."

Words fail Michelle, but the manager agrees, with a few well-chosen comments, to return at noon for the inspection,

"My moving crew is on the way, and the apartment has already been cleaned. We will be ready by noon."

The manager agrees to return at noon for the inspection. Just as she is leaving the apartment complex grounds, Michelle spies a large moving van turning around the corner. Her brother, Benedict, is behind the wheel. The moving van backs into the parking space next to her tiny car and her brother gets out of the driver's seat, holding a large brown bag containing toasty bagels and cups of hot, steaming coffee.

"I know you needed some extra motivation this morning. So, after getting the truck, I stopped at your favorite place and picked up a little pick-me-up for both of us," Benedict says with a slight, tired smile on his beard-covered face.

Michelle's frustration toward her brother fades as she grabs the coffee and takes a long, savoring sip of the welcomed, steaming eye-opening liquid. It refreshes and invigorates her, as she is tense and tired this morning. Benedict cautions her against moving from Nevada since it has been their home for over 20 years. He senses her resolve and is determined to help his sister make a move to Colorado and leave some sad and painful memories buried in the desert sand. They both take a moment to sip their coffee and rest against the moving van to reflect on recent failed relationships that may have been the partial impetus for the move.

Michelle is first to speak with a pensive voice, "We sure have made a lot of memories in the desert. Some of them I wish never happened. We did a lot of growing up here."

Benedict adds with a sigh, "Yeah, Dad dying tore everyone apart. He left us all with unanswered questions. It has been hard."

The pensive mood shatters as Dove-Whispering comes skipping down the apartment stairway holding a crumpled load of clothes while humming a tune and loudly talking on her cell phone.

"Yeah, we are leaving. I can't come to see anyone tonight," Dove-Whispering says in a sad, monotone voice as she talks with a friend on her cell phone.

Hearing this, Michelle and Benedict look at each other and shake their heads in agreement. Maybe it is okay to move at a slower-paced Colorado for the sake of a growing teenaged girl. Brother and sister head up the stairs to complete loading the van while Dove-Whispering takes her precious teen wardrobe to the car for easy access.

Noon brings the apartment manager back for the check-out, and the move is on. It is both a sad departure and a happy time.

Since Benedict and Michelle compare notes about the travel plans and each has a cell phone, they are confident about the cross-country trip. Dove-Whispering switches riding positions throughout the trip when scheduled stops occur. The trip to Colorado should be uncomplicated, but as

Michelle views Nevada in her rear view mirror, she experiences pangs of regret, sorrow, and sadness. As a single mother, she often faces challenges in life without support from a loving, supportive partner. Trepidation always frames the steps of her life. She has gained experience as an educator who lays the platform for her new career in the Colorado school district. Surviving and thriving within one of the largest school districts in the United States prepares her for professional life, as her personal life was something she was still shaping and building. As the view of Las Vegas fades in the distance, Michelle is confident that she has made the right decision for herself and her daughter.

As she views the passing countryside through the car window, the first thing that Dove-Whispering notices is the color green. Even though Arizona is still a dry, sandy state, the land does enjoy a little more rainfall than Nevada throughout the year. As the car whizzes down Interstate 15, she notices that mesquite trees and Joshua cactus begin to dot the countryside. This kind of flora is rare in sandy, dry Nevada, but becomes more evident in northwest Arizona. The sight of the bushes makes her homesick as soon as she spies them. The feeling spreads from her teary eyes, through her watery mouth, past her dry throat, and shoots down to her queasy stomach. She was born in Las Vegas, and even though she and her mom often move within the city, they have never moved to another state.

Now that they are in the car and traveling, it is somehow more than she thought it would be. The feeling within her body is trying to claw its way out. She feels as though she is splitting into two different people. The familiar skeleton is staying in Nevada, while the other moves at warp speed into an unknown world that hold her future.   She is leaving her classmates, her Auntie Anne, her Uncle Benedict, and her familiar city that taught her what it means to live in a town within a community of other people, other families. Nevada is the place where she lost her grandpa. Her "pa-pa" was in the delivery room when she was born. He was present at all of her birthday parties and every one of her tee-ball games.   They enjoyed getting her dressed up for their trick-or-treat walks on Halloween.   She loved her grandpa, and even though she was very young when he died, she still misses him.   That she would re-connect in some manner with her "pa-pa" later in her mystic life felt certain to her, but now she is leaving this happy memory place.   She stared, teary-eyed and frozen in time as though she is encased in amber, while mental visions fly from her past and fade like the desert landscape dotted with withering blooms of the cactus roses.

She switches spaces at the next scheduled stop to ride with her Uncle Benedict for the remainder of the trip to Colorado.   The color of the landscape throughout Utah just keeps getting greener and greener.   It is almost more than she can bear!   She is a child who tends to withhold her feelings from the outside world, but they seem too big to hold their place within her this time.   Maybe it is her American Indian heritage trying to handle all of her emotions, but how could she know?   She just knows that it feels very uncomfortable.

Uncle Benedict can see that she needs to talk and their deep conversation seems to help her deal with her feelings. As they approach the outskirts of Denver, Dove-Whispering feels sad but no longer overwhelmed by feelings of loss.   She knows that her uncle will be returning to Nevada after getting them settled into their new home in Colorado and she is happy that he is making the trip with them. He offers some sense of family on this sad departure day.

Auntie Anne does not move with them. She is still recovering from her recent kidney transplant. Dove-Whispering's mom, Michelle, is the organ donor for her younger sister and saved her aunt's life. It seems that everyone is willing to help and support each other whenever any of them is in need. If auntie were able, she would be happy to make the trip. Auntie Anne is planning a visit to Colorado during the upcoming summer, and Dove-Whispering is excited about spending some quality time with her favorite aunt who seems more like a sister than anything else. Dove-Whispering already misses their helpful talks. Maybe she will find a close friend living in Colorado. Since she is entering the school in her sophomore year, it will be difficult for her to find good, trustworthy friends. She thinks that joining a science club or the volleyball team can help her become acquainted with her new classmates. It will be rough being the new girl in a new school, but Dove-Whispering has faced that challenge before, and she knows that she is tough enough. She has watched the women in her family rise to challenges. These thoughts occupy her so that she does not notice the slowing motion of the van.

As the exhausted caravan draws closer to their destination in Colorado, the lights from the highway seemed to twinkle, or maybe it is just their tired, burning eyes playing tricks on them. The Colorado landscape is strikingly different from the sparse, arid flat lands of the Nevada desert. Dunes and mesquites seem to give way to tall, waving green grass and vast mountain vistas. Michelle takes the lead as they near the highway exit. She secures an apartment in a small, bucolic town south of Denver and the location directions seem harder to follow in the dark of night. They maneuver rolling mountains as the sun is setting across the highway and that seems to increase the stress across their shoulders and the sting in their eyes. Their new home will be a welcome sight.

Completing a series of twists and turns brings them to an upscale apartment complex on the outskirts of town. They pull up in the parking lot of the main office location to verify the address and check-in with the complex manager. They are lucky to find someone in the office since the business hours close at sunset and it is just half past. The main office offers user-friendly electronic equipment complete with a movie viewing room and a self-serve popcorn machine that is a welcoming sight for weary travelers. The on-site manager checks them in and gives them a tour of the front office. They learn it also includes access to the outside swimming pool. Michelle makes a mental note to use the exercise room as soon as she secures a well-earned rest. The challenge is that their apartment, located on the third floor of the complex, is a hard climb.

Benedict and Michelle drive their vehicles around to the apartment site and feel a little overwhelmed as they stand at the base of the winding staircase and look up toward the third floor. It will be another long, exhausting night of hauling personal belongings and household goods out of the vehicles and up the treacherous steps. Neither possesses the strength to endure the ordeal.

Dove-Whispering flings the van door open, races up the stairs and upon reaching the top, she turns and exclaims,

"See, the climb is not that bad. We can run up fast."

Benedict raises his hands in the air and responds by commenting about the resilience of teenage girls.

"I can't believe it. Just a few hours ago, Dove-Whispering was sad and boggy about leaving her best friend and most favorite place in the whole, entire world. Now she is happily racing up the stairs to see her new home. I guess I just don't understand the workings of teenage girls."

Michelle walks up next to her older brother and placing her hand on his shoulder, looks him in the eye and nods in agreement saying,

"I know what you mean, Benedict, and I have been working at it for a long time myself."

Exchanging a slight, knowing smile and a nod of their heads, they walk toward the apartment stairway, resigned to a long nights work.

CHAPTER 4

THE OTHER LIFE

*"CNN found that Hillary Clinton is
the most admired woman in America.
Women admire her because she's strong and
successful. Men admire her because she allows
her husband to cheat and get away with it."*

Jay Leno

Pamela Love lives in Colorado. Her ancestral family moved there in the late 1800's to expand their hotel business. Her parents were successful in developing a large, upscale apartment complex in BigTon – a small town south of Denver. The area, just outside of Denver, was surging in the development and well-heeled newcomers were looking for luxury, affordable rentals within driving distance of the metropolitan area. Pamela's parents positioned the

complex on the edge of town in an upscale section, allow-
ing for growth along with city development. They wanted
to ensure that their business would be a stalwart of the
community much like the ingrained patina of a treasured
item. She values this tradition and eagerly learns the apartment management business by both watching her parents
and working at the complex. She inherits the responsibility and management of the business after they pass "to the
great beyond." Often, she struggles to handle the sprawling
complex.

In her late 20's, Pamela is dating young, eligible men, yet
the business part of her life leaves little time for a "love life."
Her position as an apartment manager gives her obvious
opportunities to meet potential prospects, yet, her like-age
encounters all seem to lack maturity and sensibility. A new
millennium is upon her, and she hopes that a fresh century
will reveal new opportunities or relationships that will en-
rich her life. The BigTon chamber-of-commerce offers her
partnership with other area retailers, but this activity also
leaves little options for her in the way of a stable, personal
future. She meets a few of the other chamber members such
as the owner of the Insurance Consultants, Mr. Menendez,
who extends a helping hand with needed building repairs
when she first assumes ownership but enjoys the little interaction with eligible bachelors. Running a public business leaves little time to socialize, and she finds it hard to
extend herself to social functions. Most of her high school
classmates have already married their life-long mates and
are starting families. Indeed, others tell her that her facial
features are pleasant to look at and surely complements her
long, flowing, dishwater blonde hair and tall, statuesque

physique. These physical attributes do attract eligible suitors, but none offers the stability for which she is searching, so, for now, she will focus on her business and continue to maintain its strong, solid reputation.

Front and back office duties fill Pamela's days – each fading into the next. Accounting duties, tax forms, employee time sheets, supply ordering, health code adherence, and concierge duties occupy her days and nights – this is her future, she fears. She passes the next few years longing for a loving partner to help her enjoy the snow-filled mountains of winter and the wind swept, flower covered valleys of springtime.

Absorbed in her routine, she does not notice him enter the office. Paperwork and ledgers occupy most of her morning. She is just replacing an updated ledger onto the counter under the front desk when she stands up and sees a middle-aged, pleasant looking man standing before her.

"Good morning. I am traveling here on business and want to rent an apartment. It may be for a few weeks or maybe longer," William says with a sly, yet somewhat mysterious, tone. He continues,

"I work for an insurance company. I'm single, and do a lot of traveling."

She detects something unidentifiable yet alluring in his voice that gives her pause. He certainly appears unthreatening, so she agrees to show him the available apartments. After viewing each unit the intriguing man, who introduces himself as William, chose the unit which is situated closest to the management office of the apartment complex, stating,

"This will fit my needs just fine; I'll take it. I don't have too many personal belongings so I can move in tomorrow."

William is more than eager to offer an initial down payment and the first few months' rent in advance. After the transaction, he tells Pamela that he does not have a permanent address. He wonders if it is okay with her if he receives his mail here, at the front office. She thinks it is a little odd since he could rent a post office box at the local copy shop across the street, which is what most residents do. When she suggests this, he mumbles an incoherent statement about moving around the country with business related duties, and it will be more convenient for him to pick up his mail at the apartment. She considers this and decides that she would let him know her answer in the morning.

Ideas of this "William person" occupy her thoughts most of the night. She decides that even though he carries an air of uncertainty about him, he did not appear to be dangerous or combative. When a "Google" search did not locate any criminal charges or infamous history, she agreed to rent him an apartment next to the complex office and let him receive his mail there as well.

William moves in the next day with few basic belongings. Viewing this, Pamela begins to wonder about his history and job status. "Being in the insurance business," could mean anything and he never clarified what he did in that field. She decides that she will watch him a little closer than her other tenants. Something tells her to observe him at a distance before asking any more questions.

William settles into his job in Colorado. His assignment is to contact homeowners who experience damage to their homes from natural disasters, i.e. hail storms, floods, windstorms, lightning hits, ice and snow damage. He would secure work contracts from the owners for home repairs and then contact approved contractors for the repairs. William's company takes a percentage of the insurance payment for securing the repairs. He has no time clock to punch, no schedule to maintain, and no immediate boss to report to as long as the job is complete. A good situation for him, and he progresses within the business. William's knack for talking helps him relate well to people on a short-term basis and can engage them long enough to get the paperwork secured and the checks processed. He is a good "front guy." As my grandmother would say, "he has the gift of gab."

Pamela closely observes William each time he comes into the office to pick up his mail. Sometimes they exchange a brief, pleasant verbal exchange. Often, they are busy and just flash a wave of greeting with their hands. She guesses that they are acquaintances but not friends. He seems pleasant enough but not willing to share a lot of personal information. She begins to wonder about his sense of guardedness. One particular slow paced, late afternoon, Pamela decides to ask William questions about his residence before he moved to Colorado. She guesses that he would be resistant, but she wants to know this man a little better.

He is not a harsh man to observe. In fact, he is quite pleasant to her eyes. His skin now sports a crisp tan – his skin's milk-toast hue has disappeared. His head licks door arches as he passes through, although there is some thinning of his black, wavy locks. He can easily hide behind a sturdy oak tree from his shoulders down. She guesses that he is about fifty years old. Altogether, William, in her searching eyes, cuts quite a fetching and handsome figure.

Pamela is sure that William must have a personal past that he does not want to reveal and that he is indeed a ruggedly handsome yet secretive man. Pamela observes William talking on his cell phone speaking in a hushed tone while he stands on the apartment steps. He cradles the phone in his hands, and his lanky posture hovers over the phone during the conversation as though he is trying to conceal the discussion. Much like a female lion protecting her kill from a pack of circling hyenas. He is trying to hide parts of his life. William never talks about his previous life in Nevada.

After closely observing him for about six months, Pamela decides that she will approach William the next afternoon when he comes to pick up his mail at the complex office. She has no idea what to say, but an encounter seems appropriate, and she wants to know more about this elusive man with a shady past. The thought occupies her mind all morning as she busies herself with mundane office duties. The day's activities seem as though each is deep in wet, captive mud – she cannot determine why this day should be different from any other, just longer or slower.

She watches William walking up the stairs that lead to the apartment office. Stepping through the doorway, she greets him with an unusually warm smile and welcoming voice.

"Hello William, how was your day at work today?"

He is surprised at her regard since his thoughts are still concerned with the experiences of a long and difficult day.

He slows his pace, places his leather briefcase on the floor and intentionally leans against the edge of the front counter, letting his left elbow and arm occupy most of the top of the check-in desk. Necessitating that he slowly move toward Pamela thus bringing their upper bodies into close contact – his unexpected response to Pamela's greeting is immediate, firm and intense. Looking straight into her eyes yet saying nothing, he holds her attention with a warm and welcoming smile. Struggling to maintain his engaging gaze, it is obvious to her that William may want more from this conversation than she expected and she swallows hard, blinks her starry eyes and feels her body slightly sway. Struggling to bring the open windows of her soul back into his direct line of vision, she experiences her hot breath forge over her already moistened lips. It feels as though someone is slowly pouring cool, clear spring water over the dusty, desert sand dunes. Instant refreshment spreads hotly throughout her moist, shivering, body. Words and thoughts elude her. A simple sentence to a brief acquaintance sways her to her inner core.

She struggles to subdue her gaze and responds slowly, saying:

"I want to know if your new job is something that you enjoy. Sometimes starting a new job and moving to a new neighborhood can be very difficult if you don't have help."

He pauses for a moment, maintaining his welcoming eye contact and then replies," Well, I'm not married, and kids don't cloud my thinking."

She steals a quick look at his "ring" finger and finds it empty – although detects a faint outline of a ring band from a past placement. It is as though someone just whispered a quick secret in her ear and then disappears. The essence leaves her with the feeling that William possesses deep seeded secrets.

Regular encounters at the front office seem to strengthen their relationship, and she finds herself waiting for his "mail calls" where he will flash his welcoming smile. Weeks progress toward months much like the seasons of the year, with each solstice renewing their rituals and familiarity. Pamela's initial watchfulness fade and William's approachable manner welcomes her. She finds herself looking forward to his visits with excitement and realizes that when they meet, she feels different – someone is pulling back a veil covering her face, and she is viewing through different eyes. Since William came into her life, all of her senses are sharper. She notices that her coffee smells stronger than before, her telephone rings louder than she remembers, and the paper boy throws the post with more gusto, and it lands in the perfect spot. What changed? She had not taken any new medications; no one left her a large monetary fortune, no physical remodeling of the apartment complex occurred. The difference, she realizes, is a new person in her life, William Henry.

When this realization descends over her, she feels uncomfortable, yet she cannot identify why she feels this way. The main difference in her life is her "mail call" visits. Her persona split into two parts, one before and one after Mr. Henry. This new feeling is uncertain. It occupies her with anxiety and completeness at the same time. She has no extended family with which to discuss the changes in her life. Her busy schedule leaves her little time to interact with the community, and she realizes that she is isolated from society. The few people that she does associate with are other business owners through the Chamber of Commerce. She knows Mr. Menendez who wrote the insurance policy for her apartment complex, but somehow it does not seem appropriate to call him and discuss personal life and feelings. She yearns to talk with someone who can understand her, someone who can help her sort out her feelings and emotions, but alas, there is no one, no one except Mr. Henry.

William's job with the insurance consulting business keeps him busy since moving to Colorado. Contracts flood in after the recent hailstorm and flood damage. The business requires a sharp learning curve for someone who did not have a history of evaluating natural damage assessments or calculating repair costs. However, Mr. Menendez takes the time to show William the basics of the business and instructes him on the finer points of contacting clients in the method of "cold calling" after a disaster. Mr. Menendez invites William to observe daily interactions within all aspects of the company. He learns how to contact a client, present them with the guidelines of a repair package, and complete the contract. Once the basics of the job are learned, William is securing a hefty paycheck and able to secure a nice, late-model CJ7 jeep and establish a sizable bank account.

William's fifty years of life encompasses a history of adventures that lead him to all parts of the world. However, the new millennium, he thought, will pave the way for a new life. Whatever his past contains, he intends to ignore it and forge ahead with a new life, in a new city, with a new job, and a new circle of friends. Of course, this is not an obvious and dedicated announcement, but William positions himself to be available for forming new opportunities. He will use the knowledge gained in life to set himself on a new path, and one that will benefit him. He does not brood about his past, or reflect on previous relationships; he is going forward with his life. Even if he did have previous relationships, they would figure only slightly into his new plan, if at all.

William intentionally loses some weight to make himself more appealing to the business community and females in general. He always wanted to shed a few pounds and now he decides that this new outer image of himself fits well with his inner decision to re-create himself to succeed. Since he spends a lot of time out-of-doors working with insurance applicants and injured homeowners, he acquires a nice brown, crispy tan to compliment his new physique. His towering height, dark, wavy hair, and warm, welcoming brown eyes help to complete the package. He feels that his outer appearance is now coming in line with his inner psyche and will help to complete his transition into a new person. He will have no need to discuss or associate with his previous lifestyle or inner circle of acquaintances. He now feels confident that he can proceed with his life in the new millennium.

He is careful to clean out his wallet and remove any pictures or association cards that can signal a link to a previous life. His billfold thinned, it now fits into the back pocket of his new pair of Wranglers. The previous weekend shopping trip at the area mall offered some men "high-end" stores, and he can purchase a few crisp shirts that match his jeans. Looking into the full-length mirror in his room gives him a satisfactory reflection. His recent acquisition of professional leather shoes and hiking boots compliment his attire.

He has no thoughts of a previous life. He dismisses them as they occupy his mind. He has lived a younger life, but nothing is going to interfere with his quest for a new adventure. Operating on "adrenaline rushes" always works well. Many situations in life taught him that lesson. If something or someone should punctuate his new path, he will dismiss it and move on. He has removed the ring from his left hand. He is determined!

As the warm day dawns, it lightens Pamela Love's mood. She is feeling a little disheartened about her social life. Therefore, the warm kiss of the sun on her head and shoulders and a walk around the apartment complex acts as a focused, guiding beacon showing her the exit path out of a deep, dark, cold underground cave. She feels better in the sun and notices that as she spends time in the summer weather, her long, flowing blonde hair takes on streaks of white and red that seem to compliment her skin tone. It is as though she has visited a spa and surrounded herself with flowers, warm baths, and refreshing aromas. She is approaching the "big 30" in a couple of years, and sometimes it seems that bits and pieces of her life are passing too fast and she cannot reach out and grab them back.

These are fleeting thoughts as she strolls through her complex and inventories structures and landscapes within her business – which seems more like her home than a business. It is her life since her parents died and she somehow feels that she spends all of her energy and time keeping the apartments functioning like a well-oiled machine. It seems like her future is pre-determined since her parents just assumed that she would "take over" the business. It is the expected thing for her to do.

Today that future seems to fit like a puzzle into her mental plan. She can visualize sharing that idea with someone who cares for her, and she would spend her life with that person. She learned long ago that she is much like one-half of a pair of mated swans, but has not yet found her life-long mate. She feels a slight twinge in her heart. Much like a pin sticking an inflated balloon, she just did not want the air that supports her structure, to leak and disappear. Whatever the future brings, she wants someone to care for her, and she desires someone to love.

She is so absorbed in her pensive thought while standing behind the front desk that she does not notice a tenant standing in front of her. His voice is familiar, yet possesses a titillating tone, which she has not noticed previously.

"Well, good morning there, beautiful. You seem lost in your thoughts." The voice possesses a questioning tone.

Looking up, she welcomes the seductive brown eyes of William as he leans over the front counter with his left elbow resting on the surface so that his upper body occupies most of the "public space" that polite people share during a discussion. His presumptive posture leaves only a small space in which he and Pamela can conduct their conversation. His abrupt and intense approach surprises Pamela. She senses that he is secretly watching her before approaching the front desk. She senses a tingle spreading through her body. She feels overwhelmed, yet slightly intrigued by the bubbling within her stomach: or is it somewhere a little lower in her anatomy. A warm and stimulating sense spreads over her like the pleasure she enjoys while sipping a mug of steamy hot chocolate topped off with warm, sticky, melting marshmallows.

"Well, William, I didn't notice you there. You stole my breath. I am thinking about something else instead of tending to business at the front desk. How long have you been standing there?" – A little cough is interrupting her response.

His eyes twinkle. That is the response that he is looking for when he positions himself in that most provocative stance. It is becoming obvious to Pamela that this Mr. Henry is a man with a suspicious background and has no problem making his amorous intentions known. In that split second, she wonders if she needs to guard her heart.

⊷⊶

Benedict is unpacking boxes. He spies pictures at the bottom of the crate. At first, he hesitates to pick them up, especially the one of him and William – Dad. It was the one taken of them during the scouting trip when they were cleaning up the hiking trail in Hawaii. The picture, taken at the end of an enjoyable day, shows everyone dirty, sweaty, tired, but feeling wonderful. Benedict does not have a copy of this particular picture and knows that their dad gave this one to Michelle right before he left for one of his extended trips to Colorado.

Benedict lifts the photo from the box and stares into his dad's face. He remembers the last time he spent time with his dad was when he is visiting him, and he lapsed into a coma. Tears swell in his eyes, but he does not notice until he feels the small drops of moisture touch his cheeks and he wipes them away with the back of his hand. He wonders, "What were all the secrets that his dad took to his grave? Was there something in his dad's life that would have shattered the family?" Whatever his dad was reluctant to discuss, was in secrecy for posterity.

Secrets were bothering his dad on that last trip from Colorado to Nevada. Benedict picks him up from the airport, and his dad looks healthy but distracted. William seems confused and secretive when Benedict questions him about his insurance job in Colorado. His dad avoids answering inquiries such as his apartment, roommates, or work colleagues.

Michelle interrupts his somber reflection. She remarks that items need unpacking before they sleep, but everyone is exhausted and functioning on adrenaline. He agrees and places the "moment of memory" on the shelf along with the other items that would help Michelle and Dove-Whispering feel welcome in their new home.

⊷╪ ╪⊷

"I have been here long enough to learn that you are a person who often gets lost in her thoughts. So, what are you dreaming about, beautiful lady?" was William's quick, soft-spoken response.

His words cascade from his lips as though a wizard is releasing a magic spell disguised as massaging fingers filled with persuasive potions that swirl around Pamela's head and tousle her hair offering comfort and relaxation. She softly inhales as she struggles to gather her thoughts and devise an answer that seems generic and business-like.

"Well, you're right, I should concentrate on my tenants, but sometimes I wonder if managing this complex is all there is in life. I often wonder if I am missing the exciting parts of life," but William detects from the glint in her eye, that she is indeed trying to hide a more emotional response.

Reality returns when she feels a persuasive touch. Looking at it, she realizes that William has positioned his larger, protective hand over hers and she can sense that he is waiting for her response. As she feels his hand, her senses tell her that it feels good. Like a soothing gel missing from her life for a long time suddenly flooding and moistening her system. There is silence between them, they exchange sensual, inviting glances, William speaks first:

"Well, Pamela, we could start saying hello to each other every day when I come to get my mail. Then we would look forward to seeing each other every day. What do you think?" he holds her gaze waiting for an answer.

Her answer tumbles out without thought, "Yes. That would be okay. I guess. I would look forward to that. It would make me happy."

Pamela and William lightly massage the others hand before releasing their embrace. They reluctantly part, each with a developing smile, looking forward toward the next mail call.

━┼ ┼━

William is at a business meeting the next morning when his boss, Mr. Menendez approaches.

"Well, William, how are things going for you in your assigned territory? I know that you may still be settling in, but I want to make sure that you check all the clients in the area. We are looking at you as our advance man since you always seem to have the gift of gab and the one who can close the contract for our insurance company to complete the insurance work."

William rises from his seat and turns to shake his bosses hand and greet him with his usual "business" smile.

"Sir, things are going very well. I close contracts and am working in a section of town that experienced a hailstorm about a week ago. Those homeowners may not know it yet, but they all experienced roof and siding damage which I have a good eye for detecting."

William responds with his usual confidence and slightly arrogant tone.

Mr. Menendez explains, "Well, William, if you continue to produce for our company as you have for the past few months, we will be very happy with your efforts. I don't know if you intend to return to your family in Nevada or not, but if you decide to stay here in Colorado, you can have a job with this company for as long as you want it."

William assures Mr. Menendez that he intends to stay in Colorado at least for the near future and is pleased with his income. He relates he can purchase a new Wrangler Jeep and a new wardrobe. These items are fitting in well with his life in this new area and his new job. Mr. Menendez is happy to hear this and congratulated his efforts for the company.

As the two men part company, Mr. Menendez turns back toward William and asks if he knows the proprietor at his apartment complex. Since both she and Mr. Menendez were members of the local Chamber of Commerce, they know each other well and often meet within the community. William pauses as he walks away, half way turning toward Mr. Menendez and states,

"Yes sir, I know that lady, and she seems mighty fine to me." A more robust response than he expects and he shoots William a questioning glance.

William meets the stare and responds, "Don't worry, man. I will not tarnish the good name of the company. I know how to keep things on the down-low."

Mr. Menendez wonders if he made a good decision in bringing William into the established company. It is true that he is a good "advance" man and sells multiple insurance contracts for home repairs, but something told him that William's darker side would bring infamous attention to the company. Mr. Menendez is also uncomfortable with William's rather disrespectable remark toward Ms. Love, a fellow Chamber of Commerce colleague. He makes a mental note to himself that he will talk with Ms. Love at the next chamber meeting. Mr. Menendez has been in the insurance business for almost forty years, and even though he entered the enterprise in his late 20's, he feels that the business is always responsive to community needs and respectable within the professional arena. He did not want any of his employees damaging that standing within the community. He makes another mental note to watch William in his everyday business dealings.

⇌ ⇌

Pamela looks forward to the mail delivery the next morning with a feeling of giddiness surprising her. Reviewing stacks of letters with a mindless attitude, occupies most mornings. This morning is different, there is a sense of wonder in the air as if a florist just brought in a fragrant bouquet of spring flowers into the room, and everything seems fresh and new. Just as she is finishing sorting the mail, she sees William walking through the front door of the office. She feels a tingle in her stomach and then it travels, oh so slowly, to the lower region of her pelvic area. The feeling is an intermittent pulse, more than a twinge, and it stimulates a sensation that sends a charge throughout her entire system. She is sure that someone set off an electrical charge through the carpet because her feet feel like bees are defending their hive and stinging the intruder. This split-second of sensation coincides with William's approach. Her mother told her about things like this when she was a young girl, but she never imagines that it will happen to her. Mom did not describe the experience. William approaches her at the front desk and flashes his smile that he saves for those most persuasive moments. "Good morning, beautiful lady. How is your day so far? I am reading about Cheesman Park over in Denver. It sounds like a very interesting place. Would you like to take a drive with me and walk through the area this afternoon?"

Pamela, still involved in her emotions, feels herself agreeing to the tour with this most enticing messenger. Soon, they are driving through Denver and approaching the rod iron gates of the front gate of Cheesman Park. William and Pamela exchange small talk about the weather and flora and fauna within the park boundaries. He reads brochures about the history of the area and thinks that he can impress Pamela with his knowledge.

"This area was originally a cemetery," he states with an air of arrogance. He is surprised when Pamela responds, "You are right, William. My parents were friends with Senator Henry Moore Teller who persuaded the U.S. Congress to convert the cemetery into a park. The community leaders did a lot of work to complete the project so that everyone concerned was pleased with the project."

He tries to contain his surprise by continuing to read his brochure. "It says here that there was a mortician named E.P. McGovern who contracted with the city to move the bodies. Instructed to move the caskets and bodies together, instead, he dismembered the skeletons and used child-sized coffins. There is evidence that not all of the bodies are relocated or that all of the skeletons were correctly identified." William read the information from the brochure because he could not tolerate anyone knowing more than he does in a conversation. He also wanted to intimidate Pamela because it made him feel superior when he made women feel less able in a relationship, although he would never admit that to her.

This conversation dampens the intended mood that William planned for the outing. He is anticipating that Pamela will be enamored with his charm and begin a romantic relationship. He changes the tone of the conversation,

"Pamela, enough discussion about the park. Tell me more about yourself. I want to know everything about you."

He says as he turns from her side and faces her making sure that their profiles are a few inches apart – he wants to experience her breathing.

"Well," she begins with a slow, thoughtful word, "I am an only child and have lived here in Colorado all of my life. My extended family settled here in the 1800's when the area was still flush with the gold rush money. My parents began the hotel development in the 1900's. They took their portion, realized in a windfall, and started a small boarding house for the miners who refused to believe that their pot of gold was gone. Their complex grew along with the population, and within a few years, construction started on the current site. The apartment, built in stages, was completed by the mid-1990s and filled."

William stops here and places his hand firmly in front of her face.

"I ask about you, not about your life at the apartment. I want to know what you think, what you like and dislike. I'm curious about what you do for entertainment."

"I have been concentrating on running the business for so many years that I have no extra time to devote to entertainment and relaxing. My parents gave this place to me, and it's all I have."

She was staring off into the distance of Cheesman Park with a fixed, blank stare, and as she recites the details of her plain existence, a small tear formed at the corner of her eye.

William, sensing that Pamela is vulnerable, slides his arm around her waist, bringing her body toward him. He hesitates, waiting for her, accepting her response by relaxing and folding into his embrace. Time stands still, like a blast from Iceland freezing eternity. She accepts, relaxes, and collapses into his embrace. She hesitates before releasing her inhibitions, letting him know that she welcomes a complete relationship with him. Their sensual embrace and amorous kiss seals the bargain. She feels his rough, yet experienced hands massage her breasts through her delicate seersucker dress. The stroke of her nipple by his tough skin sends an electric shot through her body and arouses her cervix and vaginal area into a circus of biting ants, nipping at the edges of her inner lips. She responds by offering a firmer embrace of her trembling body, which he accepts.

"Oh, William, I think that I am falling in love with you," Pamela speaks with tenderness as she lays her head on his welcoming shoulder.

The crack of electricity from a blackened sky breaks their mesmerizing embrace. Night envelopes around them ignoring their acknowledgment. Pamela quickly feels the brisk night air nipping at her ankles. She shivers from both his internal arousal the external thermometer shift. Knowing that he has accomplished his goal, William gives Pamela a last reassuring embrace and smoothly whispers that he will accompany her back to the apartment complex.

The ride back acknowledges a change in their relationship. Pamela is in love. William is in lust.

⊨⊧ ⊩⊨

Mr. Menendez decides to approach Pamela to determine how she is handling the management of the apartment complex. He was a close friend of her parents and told them that he would watch over their daughter. He did this throughout the years, just to ease his conscience. Pamela always greets him like a favorite uncle. His concerns ease as he left each previous visit and he hopes that this episode will be the same. He always struggles with the concept of being large of soul. The idea that he can consider aspects of a person's life that are different from his, yet he attempts to understand the choices that the other person makes; especially if they are different from the one is that he would make. He takes a deep breath and stiffens himself as he walks up to Pamela.

"Good morning, Pamela, how are you doing this fine morning," he greets her at the front desk of the office with a warm smile.

She responds by leaving her position behind the front desk and tiptoeing around to offer a quick, easy hug, catching him off balance. Exchanging business-like talk, community activities, and the changing Colorado weather was their normal interchange. This day will be very different.

Catching his breath and regaining his footage offers him stability to hold Pamela at arms-length and gives her a stern, yet searching look into those familiar eyes.

"I didn't expect to be greeted by such a warm greeting," he responds.

"Oh, Mr. Menendez, I just feel so alive and healthy this morning. I guess that something inside of me wants to share the feeling with the first one who walked through the front door." She pauses quickly to regain her composure.

"William and I took the most blissful and invigorating walk in Cheesman Park yesterday, and it changed my life, and I want everyone to know and feel good like I do," Pamela said with a voice that sounds as if fairies and angels are enjoying an outdoor picnic.

Mr. Menendez takes a breath to help clear his thoughts before he speaks, "Pamela, do you like this man? Have you been seeing this man? He is a tenant in your apartment complex. That might not be a good idea." Pamela looks straight into his eyes, responding without hesitation, "I have never been in love with a man other than my father, but, the feeling of love that I have for William is intense and complete. He is someone with whom I want to spend my life. I know that he cares for me also."

It is obvious that Mr. Menendez is not going to have an intelligent, professional conversation with this love-flittering girl this morning. He makes his polite greeting and discreet exit. He enters his insurance office to see if William is at his desk to discuss the relationship with Pamela. He does not interfere with his employees' personal lives, but he feels that this situation comes under different parameters. He finds William at his desk. Mr. Menendez pulls up a chair next to the desk and initiates a hushed, personal conversation with his contentious employee.

"Well, William, I see that you and Pamela are spending time together. Are you friends or do you have romantic ideas?" William put down his writing pen, turns his body and chair toward the position of Mr. Menendez, and after swallowing and taking a deep breath, begins to speak,

"Good morning to you too, sir. My dealings are not any of your business. I give you a good day's work and bring in a lot of money for this company. I don't look into your personal life, and you need to stay out of mine." William speaks sternly with indignation.

Mr. Menendez's eyes burn with fire, and he shoots back a focused response.

"I know that you are married and have children living back in Nevada, they deserve respect. This kind of scandalous affair cannot be attached to my firm. You need to decide what you want. Do not hurt Pamela. I have known her for years, and she has a good reputation."

William stands up, crashes his chair against the wall, stiffens his posture, takes a deep breath, and replies,

"Keep out of business that is none of your concern."

The two staunch men part from the small confinement and the issue is left unresolved. William leaves the office and walks to the apartment complex for an intense talk with Pamela. He finds her sorting the mail at the front desk, and she greets him with bursting affection and obvious tenderness. The embrace serves to calm his ruffled nerves. He determines to continue his relationship with Pamela and derive all of the pleasure out of it that he can exude. He already separated from his legal wife and recognized children, so that his last refuge for love and affection is to be with a vulnerable, single, unaware woman willing to fill his days with love and adoration, and he sees no need to bother with legal issues.

This conversation sparks a staunch decision in both men. William decides that he will indeed continue a romantic relationship with Pamela because she is the perfect docile partner. Mr. Menendez resolves to protect Pamela if he can without intruding into her personal life. These decisions parlay a professional tension between the two men. William's work schedule makes him responsible for investigating insurance evaluations out-of-town. His work also requires him to spend time traveling to-and-from the work site to complete his assessments. The change in assignments means that he will spend more time away from his office and more time on the road. Mr. Menendez makes himself more available for visits to the apartment complex and attendance at Chamber of Commerce meetings to check on the welfare of Pamela. The two men's talk is the exchange of "work related" statistics.

William makes sure that time spent with Pamela focuses on their romantic relationship. He will hold her hand, stroke her arm, and caress her waist whenever they are together. Often, he will suggest that they spend private dinners at a special secluded restaurant that he finds during his travels. She will acquiesce.

Mr. Menendez agonizes about the encounter for the next few days. He considers approaching Pamela and revealing the truth about William, but knows that doing this will cause her great psychological pain. It is possible that she will not believe him and their trusting relationship is false.

He laments. What should I do? Should I let her continue with the relationship and make the decision for herself?

She is an adult able to make her life choices. I have no right to interfere with her personal life. It is none of my business. I knew her parents, but I have no duty to her. She is an individual and responsible for herself. What to do? What should I decide? What if she finds out later in life that I knew and did not tell her? Will she hate me for keeping the secret?

All of these issues cause Mr. Menendez many sleepless nights and fretful days. He decides that he will not tell Pamela what he knows but will be available for her whenever she needs him. He feels like an adopted father to her and makes a verbal promise to her parents to help guide their daughter whenever needed. This decision makes him feel a little less like himself. He is not sure if the new millennium is influencing him since he is detecting that basic moral standards are changing, or if his aging is changing his views. The entire incidence between William and Pamela Love tested his moral core. He always assumed that when presented with such an occasion, he would make the right decision learned in his Sunday school lessons. Now faced with such a dilemma, he is found wanting, and today, he likes himself a little less.

━━◦┼ ┼◦━━

William suggests that they live together. He approaches it from an economic view so that each could save money. Within two days of his brisk conversation with Mr. Menendez, William has a discrete conversation with Pamela concerning the economic thrift of combining their joint apartments into one living area.

"Pamela, it just makes sense for both of us. You know that we love each other and will be married. If we save money before we set the date, we can enjoy a beautiful honeymoon, and you will be able to pay someone to look after the hotel complex. We will be on an extended stay in our own exotic, romantic hideaway. It will ease your mind and make the start of our lives better."

William holds Pamela as he whispers into her ear about starting their lives together.

"I don't know, William, these days people still gossip about things like that, people living together without getting married. I love you and know that we will marry, I am still a little nervous about what the business people will think about me. I have been living and working here all my life. My parents worked most of their lives to set up this complex. They wanted me to be safe and secure for the rest of my life. It is important for me to maintain my reputation in this neighborhood. You have not lived here very long, and you do not know the people as I do. I have the rest of our lives to consider."

Pamela struggles to break loose from William's tender embrace, but he keeps a secure grip around her waist as she talks about her concerns.

The more Pamela talks, the more irritated William becomes. He decides that she is going to be part of his new life and there is no need to focus on the opinion of others. He keeps talking and repeats that he cares for her to see if she will give in to his charms. He can convince his potential insurance customers of his abilities, so there is no reason why Pamela should be able to resist him. Her desires are of no concern. His needs are the reason for their relationship.

William's attitude is obvious to all he encounters for the next few weeks. He is abrupt with his clients and colleagues. The cashier at the local grocery store tries in vain to engage him in a polite conversation, but to no avail. He becomes an aggravation. William realizes that the small moral conscious that still occupies the tiny corner of his soul is his real irritant. He will either have to get rid of that feeling or learn to ignore it, so he decides to ignore it.

Pamela is considering William's proposal of sharing living space. She's convinced that he loves her and she knows, in her heart, that the joyous feeling running through her is true. She spends time trying to consider her feelings these past few days. The future depends on her decision, and she senses that William will be a major part of it. These thoughts are entertaining her mind as she reviews the financial balance sheet for the past few months. Looking at these monetary forms makes her realize that the apartment complex offers her financial security and will be a form of refuge for her future, whatever her decision. Her parents taught her one thing, to keep track of the money. This main principle helped them establish their initial bankroll for building the apartment complex. Her parents started the sprawling complex by building on the foundation of a small boarding house. She watched them build their life and their business by maintaining good, honest work practices. Whatever the future will bring, she intends to practice these principles, and she knows that they will stand the test of time.

She decides that saying yes to William will start a new chapter in her life. It will bring someone into her life who offers companionship, love, and devotion. She craves these psychological aspects. She feels alone and living with William will lead to marriage. Marriage and children will form the base of a new family. She decides to tell William of her decision the first thing in the morning.

William enters the office. His work schedule changes and he is leaving town by mid-morning. He wants to pick up his mail and finish some last-minute business issues before he leaves. Pamela is waiting for him with a big smile and a pleasant attitude. She approaches him and hugs him, his response is immediate, both physically and emotionally. Her embrace is like a shot of hot tequila smoldering straight down to his swelling manhood, stimulating a tight, firm, wet response. He makes no effort to hide his physical response, and he is usually good at concealing his true feelings. He would ravage Pamela right on the spot at the lobby entrance if it were not for the presence of the other complex tenants.

"Well, William, I'm considering your suggestion that we move in together. I know it will affect our future. It is a big step for both of us. We do love each other, and so I have decided that the answer is yes, yes, yes. Now and forever!"

She says with a joyful and happy heart, and gives William a loving hug and delicate kiss; because she wants him to know that, she and her heart are both his, forever.

The physical response, which he makes sure she receives, confuses and surprises her. She was thinking of love, joy and forever after, and it is evident that the physical aspect of their conversation is the focus of William's enjoyment. She faintly tries to back away from him since they are in a very public area. However, he only pulls her closer and presses his body, face on toward her, so that there is no mistake about his message.

A slight struggle between them releases his insistence. Her resulting facial blush and embarrassment are evident to all the tenants, but none is so inclined to interrupt the interaction. Pamela quickly adjusts her hair and clothing suggesting that they return to their business duties. William slowly and sensually traces the small ridge below her chin and gives her one last passionate kiss on her alluring neck as she reluctantly walks away. Her long reddish blonde hair, tousled and sexy. They decide to move in together the next week. Pamela is confident that their marriage date is very soon.

CHAPTER 5
THE FAMILY

*"In three words I can sum up everything
I've learned about life: it goes on."*

Robert Frost

Las Vegas, Nevada is "sin city." However, it is also a community filled with homes, churches, schools, and families - all samples of a loving, growing and thriving community much like any other neighborhood in the United States. The Henry family lives in Las Vegas where the three children grow up, attend school, are active in church, and obtain their driver's license as their age becomes appropriate, and Benedict, Michelle, and Anne grow into fine young adults. Mr. and Mrs. Henry are in professional positions and contribute to the tax base that fulfills their neighborhood duties. The Henry family is a solid, happy, productive and loving unit. Mr. Henry is on the verge of retirement after serving his country in a military role for twenty-two years. Mrs. Henry is a practicing registered nurse offering medical care to military veterans in a civilian clinic. The eldest son, Benedict, obtains the rank of Eagle Scout and both younger sisters are active in the scholastic and athletic community.

An underlying secret remains hidden from most of the family members. The details of the secret compile for many years. The secret sends a slight vibration through the very base of the family structure, but the repercussions are barely detectable. The movement is just slight enough to prevent the foundations of the family structure from cementing itself into a most solid and firm piling. Much like the continuous irritation of a wound site experiencing intermittent scratching or irritation and thus not healing and the underlying vibration went unattended for thirty years.

William is unfaithful to his marital vows. It begins a few years after his marriage. He realizes that he can deploy to military duties around the United States, indeed the world, and enjoy the amorous attentions of women that he meets at those duty stations without any consequences. He believes no one will detect his betrayal and he can refine his deceitful activities well enough as to avoid detection by his marital partner. Indeed, William becomes quite good at deception and begins living a double life, one of loving father and family man, the other of middle-aged, single dude, dating girls whenever the notion seems to strike, and it strikes often.

His children and wife are content in their family life and oblivious to William's "other" life. Family routine ushers the children to adulthood and the union of a loving husband and wife celebrate multiple anniversaries. William develops the "gift of gab." A variety of neighborhood acquaintances interact with him at the local coffee stop each week, and he can always be counted on for a good human-interest story during his news report on the only television station in the city.

This mental history Michelle and Benedict carry with them as they travel into BigTon, Colorado. Each aware that since their father's death and the revelation of his hidden life, they both need to leave the confines of "sin city" and explore physical territory they consider a refuge for a new start for their family. The truth is that the family will never be the same as it was before the truth of the betrayal. Their mother remarried and moved away, and the once tight web of the family shatters as though a feral fox entered the hen house filled with mature, setting hens and feasts from midnight until dawn. The fox emerges covered in blood and feathers sporting a very satisfied expression, but no one gets eggs for breakfast. Michelle and Benedict like eggs, very much.

The challenge is to keep the memories, try to forgive the past, and recreate their family so that the feeling of the secure, tightly woven web remains, even though that feeling is an illusion of reality. Colorado offers that possibility. Michelle chose the area because many of her teacher friends recently moved into the area and they find the school system and emerging communities, welcoming. Since BigTon is a smaller city and a little south of Denver, it offers a perfect location, not only to grow a family, but there were no obvious signs of "sin city." Michelle and Dove-Whispering each need rolling hills, green vistas, walking paths, hiking trails, and clean air with which to heal themselves. Benedict is determined to help his sister with her new start as long as he can be close enough to help her and his only niece if the need arises. They are survivors.

⇒ ⇐

Moving into the new apartment is an all too familiar task for the three of them. Like a set routine of driving to new home, check in with apartment manager, position truck, beefy guys unpack and set up the bed and the couch, a techy person manages wall outlets for plugging in television and computer, Mom locates toilet paper and paper plates, and the kid manages the bedroom. Well, that was their process, and even though familiar, they are exhausted. Benedict, Michelle, and Dove-Whispering collapse, still dressed, on various pieces of furniture. The remainder of their lives strewn haphazardly in nooks and crannies around the apartment.

Morning brings reality. They find the coffee pot in the bathtub; their clean clothes wedged between the kitchen dishes and the forks. Dove-Whisering's shoes are pushed under the couch, Benedict locates his wallet next to Michelle's curling iron, and the microwaveable oatmeal packets are in the bedroom.

They approach it from a team perspective. Dove-Whispering organizes the clothes first into the bedrooms and then into the closets and drawers. She is good at the task and divides them into colors and categories. Her mom always is more flamboyant in her clothes arrangement, so

Dove-Whispering is eager to take on the task. Michelle knows how she wants her kitchen, so she sets about the task of placing the dinner plates and silverware close to the stove. She is not fond of walking back and forth in the kitchen while cooking up one of her delicious creations. Benedict cares less for these finer things and leaves them to the women. His talents fall to moving and placing furniture, beds, bedroom furniture, and large couches. Within two days, the apartment is taking shape. It almost becomes livable, and it certainly is starting to look and feel like home.

Feeling that their new apartment is working out well, Benedict decides that he will be leaving for his return trip back to Las Vegas. He helps Dove-Whispering and Michelle complete their final unpacking, and after that, he books his return flight. He is confident that after the settling-in period, his sister and niece will find that their new community is a good choice. Missing them is something that he is already experiencing, and he is sure that the feeling will only get more intense. The morning that Dove-Whispering is to start her first day at her new school, Benedict has Michelle drop him off at the local airport. The parting is emotional and more dramatic than he expects for him. He is a grown man, but he feels as though he is saying good-bye to his last, good friends. He finds it hard to board the flight for home and does so with torn feelings. He feels as though he is watching a small ship sailing off into the ocean, unescorted.

─═╫ ╫═─

Michelle finds her new teaching position at the Colorado elementary school familiar, yet challenging. The Las Vegas,

Kent County school district had been very political and bureaucratic, so opportunities presented themselves to interact with the educational hierarchy. She knows that education and politics intermingle. However, the Colorado system is solid and fair, so she anticipates an easy transition.

⚎ ⚎

The next priority is to enroll Dove-Whispering in her new high school. Michelle arranges this before leaving Las Vegas. Dakota Flats High School, home of the Eagles, is highly rated as a college prep school and the appointment with the academic counselor is for Monday at 9:00 a.m. The school records transfer and Dove-Whispering outlines her goals for the current year. Michelle's master's degree in Curriculum Development gives her knowledge of what classes to expect on her daughter's schedule. Dove-Whispering is interested in science and medicine, yet finds math a challenge. She is focusing on a degree in medicine for children's health. They both know that getting involved in extra curriculum activities is the key to easily fitting in with the school attitude.

Volleyball fits the bill for Dove-Whispering. Tryouts last for three days before school starts. The first day goes well, but by day three, it is obvious that Dove-Whispering's talents lie elsewhere. She is obviously disappointed, yet resigns herself to the reality. Her excitement level is building by the hour as she readies for her first day as a sophomore in her new high school. She knows that the current students all transferred into the freshmen class as a group out of eighth grade and know each other. Encountering

69

cliques in high school is always hard. She learns quickly to watch the group and check out individual personality traits before approaching anyone. Dove-Whispering is mentally deciding which students fit best with her traits. She is adept at "reading" people. She also decides that she will be called "Dove" instead of Dove-Whispering. She will introduce herself to other students as Dove. She will save her identity for only her close friends.

Dove picks her new classes carefully, always keeping an eye focused on college admission requirements. Her mother is the director of the science program in her new school position. Dove accompanies her mother on their classroom field trips and after-school seminars focused on science and geothermal issues, so she already identifies her interest in the field. Picking an elective class for her sophomore schedule offers two choices, art class or elemental science. Of course, she picks science before knowing all the details of the class. It will be an easy "A," which will "up" her grade point average, and that is always positive.

"I'm a transfer student, Ms. Walters. Is there a seat in front of the class?" Dove states with certainty as she approaches her science teacher in the lab during her second-period class. Orientation week continues, and she wants to make a good impression.

Surprise and wonder spread over the science teacher's face, a student with such a direct conviction is intriguing. The statement instantly reminds her of herself when she was a young teen just discovering the wonders of science, and she likens it to entering a room filled with treasures and not being able to decide which precious trinket to examine first.

"Why, yes, uh Miss, uh," she fumbles to pronounce a co-herent sentence.

"I'm Dove, a sophomore, transferring to Dakota Flats from Las Vegas, Nevada. I've been here for a few days, and everything is still pretty new." Her words are revealing less than her usual tone of conviction.

Dove takes one look at Ms. Walters and instantly knows that she is a good teacher, and she looks just like Auntie Anne, her favorite and only aunt. Ms. Walters has a good disposition, maintains eye contact, radiates a compassion-ate smile, and projects a caring attitude that tells students that learning science will be fun, almost a dead ringer for Auntie. Her hair color is a little lighter than Auntie's, and Ms. Walters is a few years younger, but Dove is attracted to Ms. Walters on their first meeting. It is as if she can still smell auntie's fresh baked cookies just looking at the new science teacher.

"Sure, Dove. Just have a seat right here in the front row. The class bell will ring in a few minutes, and the room fills up pretty quickly."

Ms. Walters's states, feeling a little professional pride in this new, interesting student.

Dove's orientation day in her new school is hectic, con-fusing, overwhelming and interesting all at once. The hall lockers have a new combination lock, which takes some orientation. She likes that each locker displays a variety of colors and easily identified. Her locker is a satisfying bright pink. Locating each classroom takes most of the first day, but once mapped, she puts a guide into her cell phone to help her navigate through the large buildings. Toward the end of the first day, Dove is feeling confident of her navigation skills and feels comfortable zipping through the hallways in-between classes. There are even a few extra minutes to sneak a smoke, and she keeps cigarettes hidden in her backpack. She will enjoy the break in the back hallway with her new school friends.

There is always that little something inside of her that whispers: "Just be a little bad, girl, no one will care." She felt this way sometimes at her old school also but it was always 'too big' a feeling, and it always got out of hand. She is sure the feeling is like being a trained hunting dog who lost its way and resists the call of the wild wolf beckoning from the deep woods, and she always feels a twinge to be wild.

This feeling stimulates memories of her "special days" in Las Vegas when grandpa would pick her up from elementary school. She is so excited because they always did happy things together, gets ice cream, listens to rock n' roll music, buys comic books, feed ducks at the park, etc. Other people would call him William or Bill, but he is always grandpa or "pa–pa" to her. Graduating from middle school takes on a different attitude for special days with grandpa. He picks her up from school to do such ordinary errands as grocery shopping, gas for the car, mailing letters, etc. Their conversation topics also change to focusing on hiding secrets.

Grandpa says, "Now, you can't tell your mom about this." On the other hand, "When you get home, don't tell grandma anything that we do today." She adores her grandpa, and so she will hold his confidence.

The trips to his friend's house are the most interesting. Grandpa will stop at a woman's house just for a "little chat." Dove-Whispering is introduced to the new friends and is given a drink and told to occupy herself with a recently bought comic book or a TV show. After the visit, grandpa will buy her another special treat and then drive her home. Dove-Whispering did like meeting all these new and interesting people, but she would like to be part of the conversation instead of reading the comic book.

Dove-Whispering and grandpa will also stop at a place that he calls his favorite watering hole. It offers a variety of sodas, peanuts, and crackers that she greedily eats since she is always hungry after a full day of school. Her most favorite visit is the local bank. When grandpa makes his withdrawals at the drive thru, there is always a variety of lollipops to choose from, and the bank teller usually gives grandpa a big, warm, happy smile as they drive away.

Now that she is older and wiser, Dove-Whispering realizes that her grandpa's special time was simply an excuse. She was an alibi for sneaky or dishonest activities. She loves her grandpa, but she is beginning to realize where she gets her restlessness or unsettled feeling. That twinge, which she always feels in the back of her head or the pulse in her heart that tells her to be just a little bit bad, she gets it from her grandpa. It is not a good thing, but it is their thing. She listens to that inner voice that whispers, ever so softly, that she must learn to control that pulse, that twinge, or she will wind up in trouble.

⊷⊶

The school science club holds interest for Dove. She can investigate theories and solve mysteries. Besides, it will be the perfect place to figure out answers to questions, and she is always asking questions. It will also offer a method of grounding her in school activities. Both Dove-Whispering and her mother moved to Colorado for a new life and new memories. The science club seems the right place to start. Keeping busy by investigating science questions might just quiet that little twinge deep within her that just will not seem to stop twitching.

"Well, good morning, Dove, I see that you are settling into school. I talked to your counselor, and he says that some of your other classes aren't going as well as science class," Ms. Walters says with a hint of inquiry.

She walks into the science lab toward Dove as she places her attendance book on the front desk amid the Bunsen burners and water spigots. A faint odor permeates the room from chemicals used the previous day, alcohol and lemons.

"I like science, so it comes easy for me. Math and history are not interesting, so it is hard. I only like to do things that are easy for me."

Again, Dove's honesty is showing. Ms. Walters senses that she will be able to detect if this student is lying or cheating. Her face holds a "detector" which will activate if either Dove is not truthful with herself or others, the kind of detector, which Dove, will try to hide but already knows is impossible. Similar to when a young child denies stealing a cookie but the slant in the eye and the crease at the corner of their mouth shouts out, "Look at me, I did it." Ms. Walters will deny it, but Dove may turn out to be her favorite student.

"There are some special events scheduled throughout the year for the science department, which I think will be of special interest to you. We have the science fair after Christmas. The finalists from each class compete at the regional level and then moves on to the state high school arena. The categories divide into definite science areas: astrology, astronomy, medicine, and physics. We usually have submissions in all categories and make a good showing."

Ms. Walters tries to stimulate Dove's interest without seeming too insistent since she knows that teens in general, often rebel if they think that adults want them to do something special. However, she detects a sign of interest in the corner of Dove's face when she mentions the topic of medicine. The class bell rings just as their conversation is becoming interesting. Dove hastily gathers her books and backpack as she runs past Ms. Walters, snatching a copy of the class syllabus as she leaves.

She enters the hallway that quickly fills with students entering from the front door of the school. They look confused and disoriented. Thoughts of her first year quickly flash through her mind. It reminds her that she is now a sophomore and knows all the ropes of surviving the politics of high school. She stands for a moment at the edge of the hallway and watches the new students. Most move as a herd of cattle led into their pens ready for auction at the

St. Louis stockyards. Dove's trained eye can spot a few exceptions, tall girls, unusual hairstyles, goofy glasses, unique body types. She instinctively knows that she is attracted to the student that stands out in a crowd. Dove knows that student will be an interesting friend. Dove spies one student as she surveys the multitude. She makes a mental note to learn more about the tall girl with the flaming, curly red hair as the girl walks around the corner of the first hallway. It is going to be a good year since Dove has already identified a potential friend.

CHAPTER 6
THE LOVE NEST

*"The one charm about marriage is that
it makes a life of deception absolutely
necessary for both parties."*

Oscar Wilde

Pamela is downsizing her wardrobe. William's attire is not extensive, but her closet space comprises only a small section of her apartment. The decision to live together is an interesting and romantic idea for Pamela since she anticipates that it will be the logical step to marriage. Her assumption, which she knew William shares, is the most direct step to their life together.

"I am just going to bring a few things over this morning. You can bring over the rest of my things from the apartment. I need to zip out to work. I've got a heavy schedule."

William hastily mentions this to Pamela as he turns to walk toward the front door. He throws a few of his shirts and trousers carelessly on to the over-stuffed chair sitting next to her bedroom doorway.

Pamela stands still, paralyzed by astonishment at his apparent cold and detached manner.

Is this sensitive man going to share her life? Previously discussing their future, during a loving and sensual embrace, Pamela is convinced that this currently emotionally detached person does see the world with the same eyes as she. Is she wrong? Is this person just having a rushed morning?

Pamela, absent-mindedly, walks toward the strewn clothing picking them up as she progresses toward the bedroom door, her mind reflects on the past few days of the whirlwind interactions with William. Has she missed something in their conversation? Is she assuming William's commitment to their future? Why is she feeling uneasy so early in their relationship?

These thoughts absorb her as she slowly walks out of the apartment, carrying an arm full of men's clothing. She does not realize that she still holds the wardrobe until a tenant, walking into the front office, asks if she is donating to the men's clothing drive.

⇌ ⇌

Pamela begins dreaming of and planning for, her upcoming wedding. Although some uneasy feelings will edge into her thoughts, she quickly dismisses the sensations as simply the jitters about starting a new relationship with someone.

She watches her young friends marry and start their families; now it is going to be her turn. She begins making her lists.

Her daily duties become lighter as though a feather duster has come into her home to complete all of the housework. She completes her chores quicker. Pamela wants to share her good feelings with her closest friends at the Chamber of Commerce. The next monthly meeting presents the first opportunity. Mr. Menendez greets her at the door and notes that Pamela seems especially happy. Although she is always a positive person, she seems to be full of excitement on this particular day.

Mr. Menendez is quick to inquire of her happy mood,

"Well, Miss Pamela, you seem to be in very good spirits this day. Have you found a large amount of money or found a long lost relative?"

Pamela, catching his eye, stops as she enters the room and happily states that she is anticipating her upcoming marriage.

"I know that we will be married soon. William is suggesting that we live together so that we get to know each other better. I have agreed, and he is moving into my apartment. I'm sure that we will be planning our wedding very soon."

Mr. Menendez pauses. He slowly turns toward Pamela, facing her. After catching his breath, Mr. Menendez hesitatingly asks a question to which he already knows the answer.

"Pamela, do you like your engagement ring? It must have been exciting when you both picked it out."

Immediately, she averts his eye contact and continues talking in a subdued tone,

"Well, I don't have the ring yet, but I'm sure that we'll get it very soon. William has such a busy schedule. He just doesn't seem to have time to interrupt his routine to go jewelry shopping."

Mr. Menendez feels a cracking pain shoot through his chest. At first, he believes that he is experiencing a heart attack. Quickly, he realizes it is the sensation of his heart breaking. Upon hearing the news of William's betrayal of Pamela, his heartache spreads throughout his chest. His legs buckle, and he visibly falters. Pamela rushes to help him as she grabs his arm.

"Mr. Menendez, the color is draining from your face. Are you feeling faint? I can get a doctor for you if you need help. Dr. Smith is here today."

"No, Pamela, I will be fine. I just need to get some fresh air and a sip of water. Sometimes I cannot handle too much excitement. Today will be the first time that I will not be attending the chamber meeting. I'll be fine after a short rest at home."

He has known Pamela all of her life. He socialized with her parents as they were building the apartment complex. They all joined the chamber together. He loves her as his daughter. He knows that her marriage to William will never, and can never, be. The girl who he cares for is going to experience pain and heartache, but he does not know how to prevent the occurrence. Knowing both of the people involved in the situation presents Mr. Menendez with mental grief, anger, and frustration. The realization and his inability to prevent it becomes aware of him within a minute of hearing Pamela's statement. He has to physically remove himself from the chamber meeting and return home so that he could filter his thoughts and decide his next plan of action. Mr. Menendez's body and soul fill with mental confusion and heartache on his somber walk home.

Talking with his wife helps him to resolve his emotional conflict. Mr. Menendez will not tell Pamela about William's other life. However, he and Mrs. Menendez stay close to Pamela and observe as her relationship progresses. They believe that destroying Pamela's illusion of love will break her heart. Their sentiments for her prevent them from destroying her life. The line between love and honesty blur for them on that day.

Pamela and William quickly fall into a daily routine occupied with quick, loving exchanges as they start their days and warm, welcoming embraces upon greeting each other at the day's end. Each conversation intermingles with small talk of the day's activities and future wedding plans. William promises her that his bank account is steadily growing and will soon have enough money to purchase an engagement ring. He seems to be a most thrifty man since he does not want to start their life together by buying her a ring on the installment plan.

Pamela's apartment transforms into a cozy couple's covenant. William quickly brings in his items, and Pamela artfully begins arranging their lives together. Each day brings Pamela a new feeling of security for which she has been longing. She begins to understand what her girlfriends talk about when they discuss their stable relationships. Pamela feels safe and happy. There is every indication that this relationship will be her salvation. A ring and a public ceremony will announce to everyone that she is finally in a committed relationship.

Pamela's body seems to respond to her satisfied mental state. Her energy level seems limitless. Working from sunup until sundown is now an easy accomplishment. A few months before she felt exhausted after an eight-hour day. Now she has extra energy for "after hours" activities. She suggests to William that they view a movie and enjoy a nice meal at an expensive restaurant after working all day. William quickly accepts this idea since he is always ready to socialize.

Pamela also notices that her hair has taken on a special shine like the golden silk of ripening summer corn in a Midwest field. She notices it, especially when she is taking her daily walk. The wind blows her hair around her shoulders and past her face showing off the gleaming sheen. She needs less moisturizer after her shower, and she thinks about the protective feathers of a preening desert warbler after a cooling summer rain. The cream that she normally uses sets unused.

CHAPTER 7
NEED FOR SUPPORT

"How true Daddy's words were when he said: all children must look after their own upbringing. Parents can only give good advice and put them on the right path, but the final forming of a person's character lies in their own hands."

Anne Frank

William meets Pamela just as she is returning from her evening walk.

"Gee, you appear a little flushed this evening, sweetie. It looks as though you have been doing a lot of rearranging of the furniture in our apartment, too. Have you found a pill or special elixir for super energy?" William is saying as Pamela rushes past.

He thinks that she looks like a wet, flipping fish desperately trying to find a nearby fishing hole. Pamela turns toward William, passing him a quick kiss on the cheek. She hesitates for a moment thinking that she wants more but the feeling quickly evaporates like smoke from a cigar whiffing into the air just before the smoker extinguishes the burning tip.

"Well, William, I seem to have a lot of extra energy these past few weeks. Maybe it is the change of season, or it could be I am feeling happy about telling others that you and I are going to start our lives together. I met Mr. Menendez at the chamber meeting the other day, and he asks about the engagement ring. I let him know that you are so responsible with your money that you did not want to start our lives together with debt. I guess he thought it is a good idea because of the very grave, a sober expression that came over his face. Maybe he is thinking about our future. Whatever it is, he left the meeting after I told him the glorious news. Oh William, I just feel so full of joy and expectation. I just know that something great is about to come into our lives."

William quickly turns his body away from Pamela so that she will not see the intensity in his eyes. He cares for Pamela. He has envisioned their lives together. Their future can be happy. His soul knows that destiny can make them a wonderful couple. Sure, Pamela is a wonderful, loving woman who cares deeply for him. He is sure that she can be a true lover and compassionate partner, lifelong. He has experienced these feeling before, feelings that he forces himself to ignore. He purges these thoughts and feelings from his existence, and it only takes a second, he has practice. However, their relationship will be superficial – "for public consumption only."

"You are alright, sweetie. Good things are in store for us. We are both good people, and we do good things. We love each other and want a life together. What more could we want?"

William feels a momentary sickening twinge quiver through his stomach but gives it no mind. He quickly composes himself.

"Well babe, I have to get back to the office. The new territory we are opening in the Southwest has damaged homes, and there seems to be a shit load of policies to write for the underwriting insurance. There may be some overtime involved at the office. I'll be back late."

William leaves the apartment, thoughts of his past occupying his mind.

Pamela starts the morning by working with members of the chamber. The upcoming health fair will be a busy affair since most of the chamber members pledge a booth. The theme is "A Healthy Community," and it will involve all aspects of public health. The local hospital and all of the doctors replied to the request with a response that they are interested. The local insurance companies are ready to set up educational booths, and the public health office readily offers to supply patient screening for blood pressure, diabetes, family planning, and immunizations.

Coordinating chamber functions is Pamela's focus, and the health fair will not be an exception. She is confident that with her recent burst of energy, it will not be a challenge for her to run the apartment complex and help with chamber duties as well. The next few weeks are a flurry of activity. Coordinating supplies and assigning health fair duties consumed every day. Pamela is working closely with chamber members but notices that she has not seen Mr. Menendez very often. She decides to go to the insurance office to see if he needs help coordinating their health fair booth.

Entering the office, Pamela expects to find an office filled with agents gearing up for the big expansion into the Southwest. Instead, she notices that most of the office desks are unoccupied and the telephones are silent. She approaches Mr. Menendez sitting alone in the back office.

"I thought that everyone in the office was busy getting ready for the expansion. William told me about things happening in the Southwest. With that and the health fair, your employees may well be overwhelmed. Do you need some help?"

Mr. Menendez slowly turns and rises from his chair. His face reveals a sense of deep thought that Pamela has not often seen portrayed by the man. She has known him since her childhood and thinks he is a kind and steady person. Someone to whom she can confide her everyday concerns and not worry about their release into the town gossip arena. Today, something is weighing on this gentleman. She gets a sense that it is something close to home, maybe something personal.

"Well, hello there, Pamela," Mr. Menendez forces a little levity into his greeting. "Yes, my employees are very busy these days. I do not know if the work in the Southwest will be that large, though. We may only send a couple of people over to get things rolling. There is some ground work to get done here first."

Pamela knows that even though this would be a lot of work for his company, this is not the true nature of Mr. Menendez's concern. She also senses that he will not tell her details of his private life. Out of politeness, she knows not to pry any further into the question. The nagging concern lodges into her mind, something she will think about and decide later after some deliberation. She quickly changes the subject and discusses superficial details of the health fair. The encounter leaves her with more questions but not ones that she can answer tonight in this place with this man.

She decides to focus on a subject that she can resolve preparations for the health fair. Mr. Menendez confirms that his company will indeed be setting up an insurance booth and will be displaying information about homeowners insurance and accident prevention. Both decide that the subjects will fit nicely into the overall theme of the fair.

Most of Pamela's days for the next couple of months are absorbed with the community health fair. She and William settle into a routine that fit William's needs. Pamela notices that she and William's stolen moments of intense passion are few-and-far-between, but she decides this is due to their focus on business and the fair preparations. Their love is strong; it is just the physical expression of it, which has waned in the past few weeks. When they finally have a free night, they take full advantage.

Pamela sets the romantic scene. She fills the apartment with soft and welcoming cushions to match her appealing sexual attire. The grocer delivers a well-chosen wine that is quickly chilled. Each of them arranges their schedule to complete work by noon. Their intimate afternoon buggy ride through a historical section of town sets the tone for the evening.

William is in an especially playful mood. He sneaks into the darkened bedroom wearing a clown outfit complete with face paint and a bouquet of balloon animals. Pamela is overwhelmed and surprised - the intended reaction. He senses that Pamela is going to initiate a serious conversation about their future and William wants to divert her attention and emotions. He wants their relationship to remain superficial and physical; long term will not be a discussion that William wants. He knows Pamela well enough to understand that if he can tap into her sentiment about the romantic aspect of love, she will forget about his long-term commitment to love. His playful manner sets the tone for the evening, and just as scripted, Pamela follows.

She rather enjoys role-playing with William. She has never engaged in this kind of lovemaking. It surprises her when she finds it seductive and titillating. The balloon animals became ingenious articles of lovemaking. Pamela pretends that William is indeed a famous, international circus clown who has performed before the crowned heads of Europe. The encounter is both enchanting and captivating. Pamela's passion renews and her anxiety calms. She knows that William loves her, forever.

The bustling sounds of the health fair greet Pamela. The Chamber of Commerce outreach team has completed preparations well in advance for a capacity turnout. All of the local businesses that focus on healthcare respond to the call to attend the function and send representatives. It is obvious that next year the fair will have to be located at a larger facility.

"Good morning, Pamela. Would you like to try our protein bars? We make them from organic produce." Pamela politely declines as she passes the first row of display tables, even though she knows the business owner is providing the samples.

"I have a lot of tables to check this morning. If I start eating everything, I will be full by the time I reach the end of the first line. I just need to see that we cover all of the safety items. It looks as though you are fine. If I get a chance later, I will stop by and catch a snack. Thanks a lot for the offer."

Pamela quickly passes along each table checking the few safety items on her list. The morning passes quickly. By noon, the preparations are complete, and the health fair is open to the public. The Chamber of Commerce holds a ribbon cutting ceremony and the doors are officially open.

Mr. Menendez greets Pamela at the front door and congratulates her on the fine job she and the advance crew has done in organizing the event. He has watched her grow from a small child into a productive member of the business community, and he is proud of her growth and accomplishments. He wants her to know that her parents would also be. She is thankful for his words.

She stands for a moment in the doorway watching the public participate in the aisles of health displays and feels a twinge of satisfaction. It has taken a lot of organization to coordinate this function, and she realizes that she enjoys working with the chamber. She also realizes that she feels a little weak and dizzy – probably due to hunger. She has not eaten since early this morning. It is time to take advantage of the offer for the protein bar. It will at least be a snack to hold her off until she can have a healthy dinner later with William.

A friend from the public health department stops her as she is heading for the exit door while eating her protein bar. The friend approaches her to see if she would like to take part in their health display.

"Well, what are you providing today? What are you doing? Checks for high blood pressure or screening for diabetes?" Pamela says with an appearance of unconcern.

"No, we are doing the initial screening for pregnancy. We found that some of our teens and younger adults are not getting prenatal care until later in their pregnancy. We decided that would be a good item to offer in this year's screening. We have had a tremendous turnout today. We have a couple of test kits left. Would you like to try?" Her friend is getting the kit out of the storage container and walking toward Pamela without concern that she may refuse the offer.

"Well, don't those tests need to be done with a woman's urine? A health fair is an odd place to do that kind of test." Pamela's voice contains a slight sense of questioning and some objection, as though it is inappropriate even to suggest something improper like this in such a public place.

"Actually, no. The lab recently developed a new DNA test that works with buccal swabs. All you do is take a cotton swab, wipe it on the inside of your cheek a few times and then place it in a reagent tube. We read the results in two minutes. It's quick and inexpensive." Her friend states with conviction.

"Sure, I'll do it. Only because you are my friend and it will be assisting the statistics for the health fair. Show me how to do the test, it's my first time."

Pamela's voice slightly betrays her with a tone of fear and distrust. She does not know of this new procedure but trusts her friend and the public health system. She takes the swab in her hand, swabs her cheek, and places it back in the tube and waits, for two minutes. Her friend has explained that the results relate two different colors, green for positive, red for negative. Pamela absently mindedly complete her protein bar, not focusing on the test results. She is confident that the tube will portray a negative result. She is so confident of the results that while consuming the last bite of her protein bar, she rises from her seat and prepares to say goodbye to her friend.

"Pamela, wait! The tube is green. You cannot go. Look at the tube. It's green." Her friend says with an urgent, yet hushed tone to her voice.

"What? That is not right! It is a new test, and things go wrong with new things like that. I do not believe it. Check the package. Check the expiration date." Pamela feels her body filling with panic, closely followed by fear. Her eyes dart back and forth, and her brain seems to fog over. She can feel her heart race in her chest. She is sure that it will burst through her rib cage at any moment. Heat begins rising throughout her neck and flashes into her face so quickly that her head is pounding.

Pamela quickly stands up from her chair, dropping the tube from her hand as it falls to the table. She frantically gathers her belongings and mumbles something to her friend about having to leave before the health fair closes. Pamela races past Mr. Menendez as she quickly leaves the arena.

Mr. Menendez, knowing her well, can sense that something is wrong with Pamela and he rushes after her. He only catches up to her because she has to wait for some construction workers to clear the entrance to the parking lot. Reaching her, he touches her shoulder and asks,

"Girl, what is so upsetting? You should be as happy as a lark. The health fair is a success. Everyone is having a good time and learning a lot of valuable information. I'm proud of you for the job you have done."

As soon as he sees her face, there is evidence of emotion that he had not seen before, and the look of terror. He could not imagine what happened to instill such a feeling in her on such a fine day.

"Oh, Mr. Menendez, it's bad. I do not know what to do! I do not know whom to tell. I am afraid that everyone will know. Now the whole town will know my secret. My whole life will be an open book. I have tried so very hard to live a good life. It cannot be happening to me. Not now. Not now!"

Pamela is rambling, and her words seem to bunch together so that Mr. Menendez has trouble deciding what she is saying. Obviously, something terrible has happened in the past few minutes, and it has affected Pamela very intensely.

He faces her full on, gently holding her by the shoulders, and with compassion and concern looks her square in her eyes and softly asks, "Now child, what is the problem and how can I help?"

Pamela blurts out her news without censorship, "I'm pregnant. The test at the health fair confirms it. It thought that I was just tired and dizzy from working too hard. I do not feel too good right now. I am going to throw up. Can you take me home?" Mr. Menendez assists Pamela to his car. The ride home is silent yet filled with thought.

Despite all of his efforts, Mr. Menendez leaves Pamela in tears. She is inconsolable. He is on his way to see William. He knows that William will be working late at the office and he did not attend the health fair. William is on the telephone involved in a conversation with his wife when Mr. Menendez enters the office.

He overhears the last few words of William's conversation, "Sure, dear, I can come home and spend a week or so with you and the kids. We can have some quality time together. I miss all of you." Mr. Menendez cringes when he hears the words whip past his burning ears.

Mr. Menendez motions for William to hang up the phone and talk with him. William is surprised at Mr. Menendez's direct manner. He is usually a very pleasant and reserved person. William quickly complies. Mr. Menendez does not restrain his anger or frustration when talking with William – their relationship passed that juncture, long ago. The message is clear, though not specific. William needs to go home and see Pamela, immediately. She is very upset.

⟞⊰⊱⟝

Pamela collapses in her comfortable chair as soon as she arrives home. Exhaustion overwhelms her. The events of the day are too big to handle. The day starts with promise and hope with Pamela surrounded by friends and associates who are willing to support her in business and personal endeavors. By day's end, she feels alone without friendly support or strong assistance to help her solve the problem of determining solutions. She is terrified!

All the stories that she had heard over the years of single mothers raising children were all about struggle and sacrifice. She was not married, and she was pregnant. She did not have a regular family doctor, much less a gynecologist. Where was she going to get insurance to cover herself as a pregnant woman? How was she going to care for a baby? Should she even think about keeping the baby? Maybe, someone else could raise the baby better than she could. She already had her hands full trying to manage the apartment complex, how could she make time for a baby?

Her brain is swimming with questions that have no answers. At least, no decision that is obvious. Sheer exhaustion forces her to bed. She instantly falls asleep. Sleep so deep that she did not hear the door open when William enters the apartment. Much like a bear in the middle of hibernation and not easily roused. William decides not to wake her. Whatever Pamela is concerned about, he is sure it could wait until they both get a good night's sleep.

William wakes first the next morning. Pamela sleepily wakes but is reluctant to begin the day with her usual zest. Pamela wants to talk to him, and he senses Pamela may have discovered something in his past. An uncomfortable position since there are many issues that William keeps tightly hidden. It is obvious, from her swollen eyes and puffy face that Pamela is tired and has been crying. William waits for

Pamela to speak. He does not want to give away a secret if he can avoid doing so.

"Yesterday at the health fair, I discovered that I am pregnant. The test was positive. I do not know what to do. I already told Mr. Menendez. Do you love me? Will you marry me?" She is facing William and intermittently pacing from one apartment wall to another. Pamela cannot contain herself and begins sobbing, again.

Upon hearing the news, William freezes in place. He knows that Pamela is very interested in marriage. That is something he is never going to entertain. However, he realizes that he needs to show compassion and support to Pamela if he is going to continue their relationship.

Without making a commitment, William takes Pamela in his arms and tenderly consoles her as she sobs, unenthusiastically saying, "Dear, we will get through this. I love you." William is mentally devising a plan in which he can continue his position in Colorado, yet not enter into a binding relationship with Pamela. He cares for her, but that feeling does not extend to revealing the truth to her. Besides, he certainly does not want the responsibility of another child. There will have to be some intricate planning to maintain this situation.

It seems obvious to Pamela that this is an opportunity to discuss marriage plans. She wants to be secure in his embrace, for William to ask her the cherished question. She is ready with her positive answer. Her body and soul are aching for the question, having rehearsed her answer many times.

Holding her gently, William is silent. She thinks he loves her and so she waits for the most glorious question.

The question that will make them one. The question that will finally make them a family. She holds him lovingly knowing that she holds her future. The extended embrace becomes the quiet answer. She knows without begging that there will be no marriage. Her dreams of wedding bliss disappear. They stand motionless in the middle of the room, he with his past and her with her future.

William breaks the embrace first with slight regard for her. "I can't stay. Mr. Menendez wants me to travel out of town on business. He has assigned me to the Southwest expansion. I leave next week. I will be back in Colorado only to make progress reports. We can talk about things before I go."

Pamela quickly and dis-heartedly turns from the encounter. Tears slowly swell and accompany the betrayal in her eyes. She cannot force herself to look William in the face, although her entire body screams, "I need you desperately, especially now." He has already made his choice. She knows him well enough to understand that there is no explanation and no words of knowledge from the man she loves. There is a shaded past which she cannot penetrate and will not try. She carries his child, a precious piece of their love and that will have to be enough.

William's icy demeanor and uncaring manner leave Pamela shaken and frightened. How can a man who shares her bed not share her life with their child? It shakes her to her soul. He is not open to discussion. When she hints that marriage is the answer to their prayers and certainly a proper solution, this man she loves, this man she trusts, turns into a cold being, unconcerned about the growing life or their future happiness.

Could it be that every sense in her body betrays her? Did the signs of caution show themselves early in the relationship? Did she choose to ignore them? Surely not. She is an educated and motivated woman who works with the Chamber of Commerce and manages her own business. How can she not see what was in front of her, a man who wants to share her bed and not her life? She is inconsolable! The feeling of disbelief spreads over her like the darkness of midnight. The feeling of everlasting exhaustion slowly and completely overcomes her body filling it totally, as though she is a ceramic mold consumed with slip waiting for the artist to fire in a burning kiln.

It is too much for her to handle right now. Her thought process is overwhelmed and chokes off. Emotions pulse her body functions. She wants to run away but does not have enough energy to lift her arms. She feels an overwhelming urge to run screaming down the main street, yet cannot speak above a whisper.

Is she going to be a single mother? Will she bare a bastard? She does not have experience with parenting and does not have an extended family network. The shame will not bother her, but the challenge is overwhelming. She envisions her skeleton struggling to hold and balance the world atlas, but her vision is not working.

She realizes that she needs help. Her first thought is to have a long, involved discussion with William. It is true; he does not want to entertain the marriage idea. What are his reasons? Before she makes any long-term decisions, she needs a plan and William will be involved, one way or the other. When he comes back from work the next day, they sit down quietly and begin talking.

William is reluctant to talk about the situation or his feelings. Pamela keeps urging since it is ultimately her life that is going to change dramatically. This meeting is an opportunity to interact with William. Support, commitment, truth and flayed-open honesty, support this stark discussion. Pamela takes a deep breath and begins slowly, stating the obvious.

"William, I'm pregnant with your child. The doctor said that I am about three months along in the pregnancy. I am feeling fine. In fact, I seem to have an extra amount of energy. From our short talk the other day, I know that you are not fond of the idea of marriage. You love me; I'm sure of that so it's a mystery to me why we can't be legal parents for this child." She feels exhausted after that sentence but sits quietly on the sofa in their apartment waiting tentatively, filled with fright and terror, for his reply, any reply.

His silence is telling in itself. Pamela knows that, but cannot read the message. Is he afraid? Does he love her? Maybe, he does not like children. William begins talking slowly and quietly, a manner she had not detected from him before. His eye contact wanders aimlessly around the room until he focuses on an ordinary looking flower vase in the corner of the room, a family heirloom.

"Pamela, I do care for you, and it is true love. I travel throughout the country and meet many people. Surely, you realize that relationships between lovers of differing ages are difficult. My business with the insurance company requires that I live in a variety of places. I never know for sure where I am going or how long the stay will be. Only yesterday, Mr. Menendez told me about the company expansion and the need for more adjusters in the field. I move around the Southwest. When I'm here in Colorado, I hope to live where I'm at now."

William's eyes meet Pamela's swollen, teary eyes as he speaks that last statement. He wants to see if the full measure of his last sentence met its mark. From the expression on her face, it is evident that Pamela is struggling to absorb William's vow.

Pamela sits quietly, studying the words that fly around in her head. She is certain that William professes his love for her. His job did require travel and that part was true. She is rationalizing his statements. She can already feel herself giving her love a "pass." Letting him off from the responsibility of providing for a family, of being the father figure for a child. She hates herself for what she is going to do and for what she is going to say. Is it true? Is she going to release him from his obvious social responsibility? Does their love mean so little to him? She can feel the pain of the compromise coming. It dampens her soul and demoralizes her spirit. It is as if a vicious tiger has just taken a large bite out of her big, bright red "happy birthday" balloon, and it pops with a deafening blast.

⊷ ⊶

After a deep breath, she sits down next to William, snuggling into his staunch posture. Knowing that she has already made her decision mentally before she speaks it. "William, I accept that you don't want to marry me. I know that you care for me, but you put obstacles in the way of our relationship, so many reasons why we cannot loving care for our child, together. I truly do not understand what thoughts must be in your head. It makes me wonder, is there some desperate secret you are hiding? These secrets will always be among us. If that is true, it is your secret, not our secret. It hides in your dark past.

The fact is, I am going to be the mother of your child. The child we have made out of our love. I cannot deny that. It is true and lasting for me, even if not for you. I already love the child that I am carrying inside my body. I will be; I am, its mother."

William finally realizes what his words sound like and how hurtful they are when he hears them restated by Pamela. She is truthful. Her belief in humans is untarnished as he has become. He lives in a shady and lie-filled, covert life filled with speeches and diversion moves designed to cover the realities of his life. A twinge flashes in his conscience, albeit, it is ever so slight, as though it were the flash of a gunshot. A question develops in his mind, is it fair to abandon this woman? She is so very close to nudging him into revealing the truth of his life. If he does expose his core, he is vulnerable. He knows that he cannot survive that revelation. He has taken such pain to conceal himself. Honesty will be the death of him.

"Pamela, I love you, truly. You make each day brighter and more meaningful for me. I look forward to seeing your face each morning. My emotions intertwine with yours. Future generations of both of our families may well remember this day. I just can't marry you." He whispers to her with all of the tenderness and sincerity that he can muster without making a lifelong commitment for which he knows she is searching.

William softens his body posture and holds her close without insisting. Pamela stands stiff and silent in his embrace. The silence invisibly entwines the couple, as they stand motionless in their apartment. The space that will soon become a family home, whatever the make-up of that family will be.

Pamela speaks first, "At least let me know that you will help me through this pregnancy. I jump between feeling tired and then am flushed with energy. My body is changing every day, and I can feel this baby moving inside of me. It scares me to imagine that being a mother is forever. I need help to get through this, William."

He tightens his embrace. "Oh, dear, of course, you can count on me for that. You are pregnant with our child. It is part of our love. I will always be a daddy. My schedule and life keep me on the move, but my love for you and this baby will be forever. That is something true." William's voice softens as the words fade between them. Each stands motionless waiting for the other's words – which never came. Their futures determined, she a single mother, he a nefarious, wandering mystery.

William leaves the next morning on a Southwest assignment managed by Mr. Menendez. It lasts for three months. The lovers exchange the promise to write often with daily phone calls. All the while, Pamela knows that the distance between her idyllic vision and her real life situation is fading.

Hotel management duties and delivery preparations occupy Pamela's life for the next few months. She anticipates the special moment each day when her phone rings signaling William's call. It is as though she is an anxious child waiting for Santa to deliver that one most "precious" wished-for gift. Each ringing of her telephone sends a shot of joy and excitement titillating throughout her body. Their conversations focus on details of the day and changes in their lifestyles when their child is finally born. Pamela's ultrasound reveals that the coming birth will be a girl. Pamela is excited but detects that William's opinion, regarding the gender of the child, is unimportant.

William's visits "home" become less frequent and shorter in duration. When he does return, his aloof attitude and obvious sense of unconcern become more evident. However, William is always clear about his affection for Pamela. Their intense, sexual encounters seem to incite convoluted discussions between the couple. William is always in an amorous mood, and Pamela's pregnancy girth prevents her from assuming the sexual positions that seem to stimulate William. Pamela begins to feel unsexy as her physical girth grows and William seems to become even more excited each time he views her naked, growing contorted body.

Mr. Menendez assures Pamela that William is busy working in the Southwest, managing the expansion of their insurance business. Mr. Menendez seems to be available to Pamela with increasing regularity. His daily visits to the hotel are always under the ruse of helping her with the Chamber of Commerce duties and hotel management items. Pamela senses that Mr. Menendez is assuming a protective stance with their interactions. She realizes that he can help her, but she does not want to depend on his support.

Albeit, support is just what she needs. William seems to be farther away, both emotionally and physically, and the pressures of life are coming closer every day. Her body is changing, and the new life within is making itself known in an ever more noticeable way.

Her ankles are swelling so that by the end of the day there is a good resemblance to large, tan colored sausages at the bottom of her knees. Her bladder is urging for emptying at the most inconvenient times, and her breasts are finally rounding out to a full cup size bigger, just what she always wanted. However, she is sure that someone snuck into her house at night and filled her with an expanding material that magically expands each day. When she looks into her full-length bedroom mirror, the reflective image is unfamiliar, gained weight relinquishes her slim waistline, is retaining fluid in every part body part and lost the overall sleek, stealth appearance that Pamela is so accustomed to seeing.

It is more difficult to perform her management duties at the hotel. Some of her friends from the chamber offer to help with the heavier, physical duties. William always seems to be away on some new business expansion project. Pamela always trusts Mr. Menendez, and their friendship has been lifelong. However, Pamela senses that he is also hiding information from her that will change her opinion of him. She cannot confront Mr. Menendez directly because that will risk that he will bury the truth, forever. That situation will create a wall between them, and that is something Pamela did not ever want to do.

She feels that Mr. Menendez is her last, true ally, and her only confidant. It is true that William is the father of her child, but he is a secretive man not prone to long-term commitments, physical or emotional. She will nurture her relationship with her longtime family friend. She will not confront Mr. Menendez about her suspicions. Like the men in her life, she too will keep secrets.

Hospital pre-registration for delivery requires that Pamela complete forms which identify the baby's mother and father, but Pamela hesitates. She and William discuss the birth, but they have not talked specifically about completing documents publically naming him as the father of her child. She needs to talk face-to-face with William. He has been out of town for the past week but will be back this coming weekend. Pamela anticipates that the discussion would go smoothly and she will return all the forms to the hospital the following Monday. She plans a romantic setting for their Friday evening meal and clears her hectic schedule so that they will enjoy eating without interruptions.

William arrives later than expected. Mr. Menendez always wants to talk about something at the last minute. The atmosphere is inviting in the apartment that the couple share, Pamela makes sure of that. She welcomes William with a warm embrace and a suggestive hug. His body initially relaxes into the embrace but stiffens when he senses that this meeting may be more than just a cozy dinner, seeing the stack of papers on the coffee table. "What's going on here, Pamela? I thought that we were just going to have a nice, romantic meal together. You want me to look at papers or sign something. Why didn't you just call me on the telephone? You did not have to make up some ruse about wanting to have a romantic dinner. This kind of thing aggravates me. Why can't you be honest with me and do things the way I like to have them done? Well, what is so all fired important that we can't talk about it on the telephone?" William abruptly brakes their embrace and briskly walks over to the table and shuffling the stack of papers.

Lowering her head and speaking softly, Pamela answers slowly yet distinctively,

"William, the papers from the hospital require that the father's and mother's name appear on the pre-registration form. I brought them home because I want us to discuss it. We have not had the opportunity to do that. I understand that for whatever reason, you will not marry me, but surely, you do not want our baby branded as a bastard or a fatherless child coming into this world. It is hard enough for a child to make its way in life, but to put that added burden on a newborn is unforgivable. I was just going to fill out the form myself, but then I reconsidered and thought we should talk about it."

William walks away from Pamela and is standing by the window on the opposite side of the room staring out into a starlit sky. The room fills with a long, silent, confessional pause that seeps into every waiting crevice. Pamela waits silently for what she fears will come. The silence continues and thereby takes on life and an answer of its own. Much like choir members who inhale a deep, expanding breath fortifying themselves for a litany of the song.

Clearing his throat, William speaks softly at first, but after the first few words fall from his lips, the following sentences ramble out by themselves. His speech is so rapid that the recitation becomes senseless. William finally turns toward Pamela, takes her by her shoulders, swings her around so that they are face-to-face and looking into her eyes, he slowly and deliberately repeats;

"You can't put my name on that paper. I have done things in my life that are not very good, and I do not want people to know about them. If you complete the form, it becomes a legal document, and then anyone can find me. Don't you understand? I do not want anyone to know the personal details of what I do. The kid will just have to live with it. You and I know the truth, and that will have to be enough."

He releases his firm grip on her and walks out of the room quickly scattering the bundle of papers haphazardly onto the floor.

Well, there it is! Pamela feels as though she is adrift, alone at sea in a floatation device, man-eating sharks surround her with only one day of food and water left in her survival kit. He is not going to support her or her child. She will bear a bastard child. The man she loves is morally weak and emotionally unavailable. She is a pregnant, single woman who will soon have another little person to support. At least, William is honest, this time. He is not going to marry her or publically recognize her baby. What is she to do? It is all too exhausting. Her brain, which usually works very well, just simply will not give up the answer. She will have to dig for this solution.

Mr. Menendez is the first option that comes to her mind. He has rescued her on previous occasions and is always honest. Surely, he will at least physically protect her and, at the very least, guide her toward the day-to-day steps that she needs to take as her delivery approaches. Her her brain races to decide what she will tell her life-long friend. Pamela finally picks up her phone and calls him. Their conversation is emotional and detailed. As she hangs up the phone, ending her side of the conversation, debilitating fatigue spread over her body, and her head fills with a splitting pain. Pamela shuffles to her bed and falls exhausted onto the overstuffed mattress. She sinks into its welcoming softness, sleeping in the clothes she had donned for the "special" dinner.

Pamela is vulnerable, that is obvious. She and Mr. Menendez talk at great length the next day. She needs to make dire changes if she is going to provide for her new life with her young child. Her love and passion for William are true but raw; she knows it down deep in her soul. She also knows that he is not the provider she needs at this point in her life. The agonizing, real world has shattered since William refuses to acknowledge her and their child. Realizing a new life is difficult, almost overwhelming. She needs courage. Most of all she will detach herself emotionally from William, the most challenging part of all.

Although William will be quite comfortable continuing their romantic interludes, Pamela fights against her conscience to consider the possibility. She does love William but realizes that he is indeed a nefarious wanderer. After great mental turmoil, it is clear. Pamela will raise their child and William would be welcomed into her life as a sometimes lover. Her humanity fades that day. Most of the inner aspect that makes her herself, surrenders, she will always love William, but she can never live with him.

The decision is perfectly acceptable to William. He can continue to travel and yet enjoy the short luxury of home life during his brief visits back to Colorado. He will be a kind of generous uncle for the child. Although, both he and Pamela do plan to inform the child when it becomes old enough.

The pregnancy progresses without complications. William seems to be out of town most of the time. However, Pamela does enjoy the friendship and company of her Chamber of Commerce friends and, of course, Mr. Menendez. The hospital registration form indicates that the father's name is "unknown."

The delivery day arrives. There was a flurry of activity at the apartment complex as all are waiting for the delightful day. Pamela's hospital bags are ready and placed into Mr. Menendez's car. Friends from the chamber call the doctor and hospital to alert personnel as to her arrival. Tenants at the complex take over their temporary duties of managing the apartments. William indicates that he will arrive later, even though Mr. Menendez knows that William is in town.

A beautiful, healthy baby girl is born that day following a few hours of intense labor. Fingers and toes wonderfully in place with color as pink as a fresh blooming rose. Her cry is lusty and clear, announcing her arrival to all. Pamela is recovering well from the delivery and returns home in one day. Looking at the precious face of her newborn daughter and feeling the warm flush of maternal love wash over her, she feels as though she baths in the springs of a natural healing pool. Pamela is now a mother, something for which she has longed.

Picking a name for this child may be difficult. Her own mother's name is Dacia, but she has no idea what name William will consider. She ponders about talking with him concerning the naming of their daughter. Naming the child is a special event and something that will stay with her, forever. Pamela finally decides that since William did not agree to have his name put on the birth certificate, he should not have the privilege of naming his child. Dacia Henri' Love is her name. Dacia for Pamela's mother, Henri' for William's memory and Love because the girl is now part of Pamela's family, a family of two.

Holding Dacia in her arms, Pamela methodically rocks in the chair her mother used when she sang the same familiar lullaby. She knows that her daughter possesses the ability to face challenges life presents, hearing her clear, lusty cry in the delivery room is evidence of that. Pamela senses that William will not be a consistent presence in this child's life, but she wishes that her daughter will know that her father loves her as Dacia dozes in her embrace.

CHAPTER 8
REVELATION AND ACCEPTANCE

*"The events in our lives happen in a
sequence in time, but in their significance,
to ourselves, they find their own order
the continuous thread of revelation."*

Eudora Welty

Two days later, William comes to the apartment to see his daughter. After urging by Pamela, he approaches the crib, picks her up, and holds her. He cuddles the baby as though he is familiar with this kind of thing. Pamela marvels in the scene, an older, single man with a natural maternal instinct. She takes a mental and physical picture of the scene. It is the first photo in Dacia's baby book. William starts talking softly to Dacia in baby words using a melodic tone that seems to calm and settle her. William is at ease holding a baby. The two, child and father, sway in unison to the rhythmic tune. Pamela slowly walks away from the pair thinking that they need to bond. William is not aware that Pamela left until Dacia begins to cry, half an hour later. Pamela knows this particular cry- she is hungry. Since Pamela is breastfeeding, her breasts are already leaking. She hopes that the front of her shirt is not betraying the response. Pamela crosses her arms to cover her breast to decrease the flow. However, the more Dacia cries, the more Pamela's breasts respond. It is time for the baby to eat.

With a rather urgent tone in her voice, Pamela says,

"I think that she is hungry. I am breastfeeding, so I need to be with her. She eats very well, but we are still getting used to each other."

Speaking softly, she approaches the couple and gently takes Dacia from William's embrace. Pamela does not recognize a look. It is almost a maternal yearning, or a faraway longing, for something lost. Pamela hesitates and considers asking about William's thoughts but lets the moment pass. Something tells her that she would not like the answer. The moment with the three of them together, seems perfect to her, very much as she imagines. There will be no risking of truth. William's reluctance to maintain eye contact breaks the moment.

William releases his hold on Dacia, all too willingly. Giving her a small peck on the cheek as she passes into Pamela's' waiting arms. He notices that there are two stains on the front of Pamela's shirt. He guesses the fluid. He had seen it before on his wife's clothing when she was breastfeeding. His older children breastfed and he remembers that sweet, bland smell of mother's milk. William quickly turns away from Pamela's direction and clears his throat, pretending to need a drink of water.

Pamela notices that William sees the moist patches on her blouse but makes no mention of it either. However, she notes that William has that longing look in his eyes, again, the same one she saw a few minutes earlier. Pamela knows, with every sense in her body that William has been in this type of experience before. She does not have the courage to confront him, not now, not on this special day.

"Well, Pamela, she certainly is a beautiful baby. Is she healthy? Did you have any problems with the delivery?"

William asks with only a slight tone of concern as if he is forcing himself to voice a pleasant interaction. The maternal, nurturing look, which was in his eyes just a few moments before, disappears. It is replaced with a tone of apathy and coldness. Even the caring sense, which Pamela saw with their first meeting, is gone.

"I'm going to be working out-of-town on assignments from Mr. Menendez, so I might not be able to spend time with you and Dacia. I like you both but cannot be attached. Moving around keeps me busy. In fact, I am moving into another apartment that Mr. Menendez found for me. It is either going to be closer to the Colorado state line or up in Tahoe, Nevada. My work determines where I live. I will be moving out tomorrow. Besides, you need more room now that you have a baby in your life. They do require space. I'll be back tomorrow with some diapers and other baby things to help you get started." William says as he turns and walks toward the door, gripping the handle.

Pamela slowly walks toward him placing a kiss on his cheek and softly placing her hands on his shoulders, knowing in her heart that their amorous relationship is ending. He will now be a shadow. She speaks with heartache; "William, you should come and visit as often as you can. That way Dacia will see you on a regular basis and have you in her life. You can watch her grow and experience some of the milestones with her. She will think of you as an uncle, or if you want, you can be her dad. It might be hard on both of you, but it will be good for her to have a 'dad figure.'" Her calm voice almost betrays her inner explosion of emotion and the implosion of her heartbreak.

William's expression echoes his long pause as he looks at Pamela. He did not expect her to be understanding. If he did not have to make a commitment, he was all in for the relationship.

"Sure, when I'm in town, I'll be visiting on a regular basis. We can decide what my relationship will be with Dacia when she gets older. When she is little, it will not matter too much. If she starts to ask when she gets older, we can just say that Dad is out of town a lot. That should work for everyone."

Pamela agrees since she thinks that it will be best for Dacia. So their life continues for the next few years. Dacia grows into an age when it is time to enter kindergarten. Although she has a loving relationship with her mother, Dacia becomes very curious about the man who periodically visits their home. William is her uncle but sometimes her dad, and it is a confusing situation.

Entering second grade brings more scrutiny from her classmates. The kids keep asking her where her dad is when "parent day" comes at school. She always responds that he is out-of-town on business, even though she has no idea what that means. It is just what her mom keeps telling her.

Finally, as she is graduating from eighth grade, Pamela and William approach her after the ceremony. Both are in a somber mood. She sits still in her chair facing the two people who have been in her life since her birth. Her mother starts speaking.

"We have something to tell you sweetie that will help you as you go into high school. We only want to make you happy and your life better," William adds, "I always love you, and now that you are going to high school, you are entering a new phase in your life. I want you to be confident in every part of your life."

Dacia feels as though she is sitting in a movie theater viewing the latest blockbuster film waiting for the climax of the picture. She cannot imagine their conversation. Her life is good, surrounded by people who keep her safe and secure. It sounds like they are about to tell her something terrible, possibly someone has died or been in a terrible accident.

Pamela finally situates her body so that she is face-to-face with Dacia. Taking a deep breath, she blurts out her next sentence with a sense of tension and apprehension.

"William is your father, Dacia! He and I discussed this at length when you were young and decided that it would be best, for you, to wait until you were old enough to understand the relationship. He wanted to be in your life as you were growing up so that you would know him as a person."

Dacia sits motionless, facing her parents. Attempting to decide in her mind what these two people in her life just revealed to her. She is much like her mother in that her emotions tend to rule her brain. However, she possesses a rough, sharp corner to her personality and she recognizes that trait as belonging to her father. Struggling to answer her parents' announcement fills her heart and brain with confusion, and questions flood her psyche. Many of which remain unanswered. She knows that they expect an answer or at least a statement from her.

"Well, I don't know what you want me to say. I always wondered about William. You never really said who he was or what his connection was with our family. He is always a shadowy figure. I thought that Mr. Menendez is closer to us. I do like you, William, I am just not sure that I can think of you as my dad. There is a lot going on in my life right now with graduation and high school starting in a few weeks. Thanks for giving me the news. I just have to think about all of this. Are you going to stay, William? We can talk about things if you want. That would be cool."

Suddenly, Dacia feels as though she might be the adult in this whole messed up situation. She does not know if she is angry, hurt, confused, or what. Certainly, it is the worst day of her life to learn this information, her graduation day of all things.

Dacia looks suspiciously at her parents across the table, and she can sense a feeling of distrust building between herself and them. They have kept a secret from her for many years, and a secret that may affect the rest of her life. How can she trust them in other matters?

She is a young woman full of energy and vitality. Her outer appearance reflects her inner personality. Her tall stature and willowy presence is a base for her long, curly, fiery red hair and piercing green eyes. Her facial freckles even seem to become more vibrant with her changing mood. Her mother gave her the logical and understanding portion of her personality, but her father's contribution of intensity, risk taking, and tendency to disrespect established limits create an inner conflict within her ability to walk the accepted paths of society. Such a combination of traits makes her an inquisitive and adventurous person but often keeps her from expressing herself in logical and understandable terms. A frustration for her when attempting to sort out or decide emotional situations such as this, truth issues about her family.

Why did her parents keep the secret of parentage from her for so many years? Is there something else to the story that they are keeping as a secret? Can she trust her parents about other issues? Did she secretly suspect that William was her father all along? Oh, the questions just flood into her head. The possibilities are so overwhelming that she has to quit thinking about the matter.

She slowly inhales and looks questioningly at William. With a rather sly and disrespectful tone, she says,

"So, are you going to be my dad now? You have been around long enough to know everything about Mom and me. One day you are just a friend of the family and the next you are my dad. It's hard to think about."

A sense of anger rises within her as she talks. The feeling does not seem to come from hatred at her parents; it comes from being denied the truth for all these years. Life surely is getting confusing on its own, and now her parents tell her the biggest secret of all, she does have a dad, and of all things, it is a man who has been in her life since her birth. She wonders if her mom is even her mom. Is this her parent's way of telling her an even worse truth, she is adopted? Again, it is all too much. She does not wait for William to answer. Her only escape is to dash out of the room and into her reading sanctuary. There she can open her science books and escape into her own, private world. The world made of facts and tested theories, hard, realistic ideas accepted by intelligent professionals. Science always gives her relief from the emotional turmoil whirling around her. She can believe the facts of science.

Relationships with her school peers also seem filled with tension and unknown nuances. Dacia often misses the true meaning of these little secrets, and it causes her to wonder, and worse of all, ridicule from the exact girls she wants to be her friends. This same type of emotional garbage always seems to be swirling around her parent's relationship. She cannot quite understand their relationship, love or lust, commitment or casual acquaintance. Nothing with them ever seems to be clear and honest.

Yes, she feels the tears swelling in the lower crevice of her eyes. They are filling the creases like an overflowing river swelling after an early spring rain. She knows "it" is coming and it will betray her. She can hold back no longer. Throwing her favorite science book against the wall, she flops down on her bed and begins giving in to the swelling tears.

She also is trying to deal with all of the physical changes she notices within her body. Recently, nothing works right.

Her hips are getting larger. Her chest is developing "buds," and she is the butt of jokes. She also notes that small shafts of hair sprout up in places on her body that should not have hair. Her skin is lightly colored, and the body hair is toasty red, so it is not very noticeable. That is not the problem - it should not be there! The past year has been emotionally and physically difficult for Dacia, and now she is learning the truth about her father.

It is turning into a sobbing escapade that ushers in the final release of an uncontrollable episode of fist shaking and fluid release from every orifice above her neck. Her ears ring, her nose is exuding streams of fluid and snot. Her reddened eyes swell into the size of plump, purple grapes near their prime, revealing only a sliver of sizzling green as she tries to open them and locate her favorite pillow. She does not often give in to her emotions. She hates to admit it, but this emotional tantrum is probably from her father's side of the family.

The summer months for the Henry "family" is a time of resigned acceptance. William moves into a new apartment he rents from Mr. Menendez. It is located close to Pamela's apartment complex so that he can visit her and Dacia when he was in town. His attitude and demeanor seem to soften toward interacting with Pamela and Dacia. Initially, their relationship is strained and curt with short interactive periods muddled with superficial talks about the operation of the apartment complex and Dacia's school activities. He feels that if he relaxes in his interactions around Pamela and Dacia, they will draw him into a familial situation that he does not want. However, as the week's progress and he maintains his staunch personality, the two women in his life relax their attitudes. Slowly, he begins scheduling visits to their home without feeling tense or anxious. Eventually, the visits are unscheduled and irregular with pleasant results. William is always a risk taker and did not focus on how his presence within this triad affects others. If it is good for William, it is good. That is not to say that all are on pleasant and familiar terms, but interactions are conversational. William is not going to occupy the position of dad and husband. Making long-term commitments just is not in his personality.

Pamela is still struggling with the loss of her lover. There is the talk of a "forever together" life between them, and obviously, that is not the case with William. Seeing William on an intermittent basis seems to reopen her emotional wounds that still are not healing. She still cannot understand why she picks a person to have a relationship with, who will not commit to her. She fell in love with him early in their relationship, and for her, that means that he will be in love with her forever. It takes a long time for her to realize that William sits differently in the world. She still is struggling with the idea. She knows that William sees more of the world. It is more than just having a wider view of the world. He has a different view of human beings. She is beginning to accept the idea that William sees the world differently. It is a difficult realization about the man she still loves.

Although, she does have to admit that she is more mature since meeting William. He forces her to examine her views and feelings about the world. He challenges her to mold opinions into a viewpoint, although, he performs this by default. Pamela sees the shadowy side of life through William. The dark side that she does not consider before meeting him. There is not a consideration for her to treat others badly or to interact with her community and not make a commitment to it. At first, these are foreign ideas for Pamela because she does not know that people interact simply for their gain. She likes her job, interacting with her business environment and talking freely with her friends; this is the way to act. It never occurs to her to be separate from the people who love and support her, to take advantage of them. She now accepts his idea that taking advantage of people is a part of life.

Her old feeling of vulnerability is creeping into her life, and for a good reason. She is a single parent. Also an independent woman dependent on the general economy. If economic times get difficult within the area, fewer people will be able to afford their rent, and she may lose some tenants. Less rent decreases her revenue. Her parents gave her the apartment complex, but the management of it is her livelihood. She does receive some support from William, but her pride prevents her from depending on that income, as frugal as it is.

Pamela however, realizes that she can control her destiny. Her relationship with William is forcing her into that position. Not only is she growing into a strong individual but also Pamela is on a threshold, on the precipice of being a wise, independent parent of a young girl trying to make her way in the world. Her daughter is quickly becoming aware of the larger world outside of their small community.

She knows that Dacia will turn to her as she encounters difficult situations and Pamela wants to be able to guide her in the right way. The way in which Dacia can make the best choices for herself. Pamela realizes that even as a grown woman, she is naïve in the ways of persuasion when a man of devious intentions comes into her life. She also realizes that she can be too trusting of people, in general. This open acceptance brings conflict into her life. Pamela does not want her daughter, Dacia, to enter into a similar situation. She wants her daughter to be able to face the adult world with confidence and personal strength that comes from thoroughly knowing herself. To do that, Pamela has to know herself and figure out complex emotional situations to benefit herself. She is working on that situation harder than she ever did before.

Pamela finds allies in her quest. Her friends in the chamber are quick to form a protective web with her to offer education and support when needed. They organize a personal defense class at the chamber office. Gender specific sections fill the requests of the attendants with all age groups. Certain business leaders become financial trainers at the local Y.M.C.A. The local police department provides gun safety classes. Pamela becomes the leader of the community watch organization.

⟫⊹ ⊹⟪

The summer months bring changes to Pamela, William, and Mr. Menendez. William's place of residence is now in another apartment outside of Pamela's complex, and he sees her less often. Mr. Menendez schedules William out-of-town more often to help with the business expansion, extended trips for William. Phone calls from him to Pamela come less often. Although, each phone exchange overflows with expressions of endearment and reaffirmations of their relationship. Infrequent, endearing phone conversations seem to be the arrangement for the near future.

Living arrangements for Pamela are not quite so drastic. Simply cleaning out bedroom closets and rearranging furniture completes the goal. William leaves some pictures and mismatched socks in her dresser. She puts these into a small box to save for his next visit, assuming that he wants the remnants of their relationships. Arranging her clothes in the closet gives her a surprise experience. Moving her dresses aside, she can smell William's physical scent. The movement of the clothes stirs the air and stimulates his masculine essence. For a moment, closing her eyes, she imagines that life returned to an everyday process a few years ago, before motherhood, experiencing life as a young, single, naïve girl. She wants her dream lover to put his full, strong manhood softly down on her. She senses that his lips are softly touching hers and leaving just a hint of his mouth moisture on hers so that when she licks her lips, she can still taste his essence. A heavy exhale from her engorged lungs causes the moment to linger and then pass.

Opening her eyes reveals the stark reality of a closet filled with only her clothes that are a few sizes larger than she remembers. She feels an overwhelming urge to jump into the closet, close the door and wrap herself in the past. This feeling to catch the past quickly fades but leaves a faint lingering in the air as though a ghost entered the closed cubicle and whispered, "It's okay. I understand the longing." She feels as though a good and trusted friend just visited and is willing to stay if invited. Her knees buckle a bit, but the experience gives her peace.

Dacia spends time reflecting on information she learns these past few months. She is fatherless or in a kind of limbo of her parentage. Obviously, she has a dad but who is he? Where does he live when he is not with her? Why doesn't he come to see her? What is wrong with her if he does not want her? All these questions keep swirling in her head ever since she can remember. Her mother is vague about the subject. She feels loved; she just has a sense of having an inner void in her life. Where does she get her flaming red hair and green eyes? Does she have her father's personality or is she like some other family member? All these ideas occupy her thoughts since, forever.

She thinks that her family is now complete, Mom, Dad, and daughter. What surprises her is that her father is already in her life. He sees every stage of her development. He witnesses her early birthday celebrations and holidays events. She guesses that this is what is causing her the most concern. Her dad is her shadowy uncle and now is taking a different position in her life. She thinks of him in a certain category, and now he needs to be re-categorized. It is like playing a memory game, where you commit a card to memory. You try to recall the picture on the other side so that you can match it when the next card occurs, and it takes skill and practice.

What she needs is time. The more she thinks about it, the more certain she is of the answer. Thinking of William as her dad is a new idea. She can get comfortable with the change, not now, but soon. The inner, confusing void is not quite so big when she thinks of it that way.

Her parent's relationship is still confusing. That, however, is another subject for another day. She is tired of doing so much thinking. It is bedtime.

However, when Dacia wakes the next morning, she finds that thoughts about her parent's relationship still occupies her mind. From all that she sees and from the discussion that she overhears between them, William and Pamela are not going to marry. That means she is not going to have a father. Although she knows that William is her dad by blood, there will be no public announcement. Her dad will not sign the birth certificate because he is hiding something. He is vague about his past and refuses to add details when questioned by Pamela. Dacia knows that her dad loves her, but he is not a strong man, not a man who can hold a confidence.

She struggles to recall her first memory with William. After moving aside the cobwebs from her past, she focuses on an incident in a room that she now knows as her mother's living room. She is young, probably two years of age. Her mother is holding her and singing. They both are swaying to the melody when she senses the presence of someone else in the room. When her mother changes the direction of her movement, Dacia notices the other person is also singing the same tune; it is William. He is not close to them, more like a background, shadowy figure. They finish singing the song, and William silently leaves the room. Her first memory is not historical, just a thought. Dacia remembers William being at some holiday celebrations, yet absent from school activities. He is a "sometimes" presence. This vague legacy of "Uncle" William in her developing years leaves Dacia with an edgy feeling toward her father. She wonders, "If he is going to be in her life why can't he tell the truth?" She endures situations of abuse from her peers because they know she is vulnerable about the situation of her parentage. People are cruel when they detect weakness. The relationship with William has taught her that lesson.

She is not sure but thinks that William is abusing her mother. He puts Pamela in a situation where she bares the stigma of single parenthood yet is expected to be available when William comes to visit. She reads a story about a "kept" woman. The main character is a single mother who appears to be an independent woman of the world, but in reality, lives a subservient life under the rule of a dominating partner. The similarities between the story and Dacia's real life situation makes her shiver. She knows that her living situation is not ideal but sees no release, as her mother makes the major decisions in her life. Pamela did not seem inclined to shift their environment anytime soon.

All of this reminiscing is useless. The past few years William is less of a presence in their lives. His out-of-town trips for the insurance company have become more numerous and extended. Mr. Menendez tells them that the business is expanding into other areas and William is the "advance" man. That means he travels into natural disaster areas that experience hailstorms, floods, mudslides and wind disasters. These are areas of danger and chaos. Her dad seems to enjoy things he can assess, make a decision, and then move on to the next assignment.

Dacia wonders if Mr. Menendez put her dad on these assignments intentionally. They keep William away from home. Then she quickly decides that is a very foolish thought. Mr. Menendez is a family friend, really more like a grandpa. He has been in her life and her family's life, forever. Certainly, he will not do anything to hurt their family! The pressures of the job must keep her dad away from home. It has been a very, very long time since she has seen him. He missed her last two birthdays.

Wherever her dad was, she hopes that he remembers the day they went shopping to buy a special present for her mom's birthday. Pamela likes flowers and feminine things. Even their home resembles a "bouquet." Colors including purple, blue, yellow, pink and green seem to be everywhere in their environment. Well, William certainly is not prone to pick these colors when buying something special for Pamela. Since it is her birthday and both Dacia and William are buying a gift for Pamela, they decide to shop together.

Dacia wants the present to be of fine quality and something that her mom would choose for herself. That way Pamela will truly treasure the gift. Dacia can sense that her dad is, as they say, "along for the ride," just to make things go smoothly in the gift buying department. Dacia knows this but wants to convince her dad to get the idea that they can spend a day together and find just that special gift for her mom. The conversation in the car traveling to the shopping mall starts with a superficial conversation.

"Dad, I'm glad that we're doing this together. Mom will like whatever we pick out. We do not get a chance to do things like this. I like it, a lot! We can say that the gift comes from both of us or wrap two different presents. What do you think?"

Dacia speaks with excitement as she is riding in the passenger seat of her dad's somewhat business-worn car. She tries to adjust the seat position so that she can find a comfortable spot but that function gets lost somewhere between the job in Nevada and the proposal for California. She did her best to turn her head, so that eye contact occurred with her dad, and that job always falls to her.

While staring at his stoic profile, she waits for her dad's response. True, he focuses on the business of driving, but a passing glance to acknowledge their involvement would be nice. Without making a quick sideward nod, William speaks with monotone syllables,

"Sure, honey, we always have a good time. We will find something that your mom likes. This mall has a lot of stuff to look at."

William robotically turns the steering wheel and parks in the first available space on the first floor. Dacia quickly hops from her seat, slams the door almost shattering the glass, and races around the back of the car so that she meets William as he is locking the driver's side. She reaches up to grab his large, rough-skinned hand, holding tight, noticing his limp grasp. She is with her dad at the mall, and they will have a good time. She can still remember the feeling of excitement rushing through her small body on that day as they walk through the automatic opening doors, hand-in-hand, father and daughter on a mission to find just the right gift to express their feelings.

Again, thinking about these situations was overwhelming and her only solace was to focus her piercing, green eyes back into her science books. Flipping her long, curly, fire-engine-red hair back across her forehead, she considers that when the summer is over, and high school begins, she will pick elementary science as her first subject. The subjects of psychology and sociology are hard subjects for her to understand. Science and numbers, however, give her a sense of concrete firmness. She can easily deal with that. Whatever high school holds for her, she is ready. She will attend the same school that her mother attended. Most of her fellow students are residents, so she feels confident that her classmates already know of her personal life. She can surely handle that aspect.

She dealt with those issues all through elementary school. Most of the incoming freshmen know her family composition, and many of those students question her parentage at every school function. Therefore, she does not expect any surprises in her interactions with her high school classmates. She also feels sure that other peers are probably experiencing similar parent situations but are less public in their knowledge. No one will willingly tell their neighborhood friends that there is a question about the genetic background of their family. If she learns further information about her family during her high school years, she can deal with it. Her relationship with her father is a

view into the raw and shameful side of life. That relationship initially hurt her but also revealed that even people,
who should love you, often hurt you. Science is facts and
hard information; those things cannot deny you.

CHAPTER 9
LIFELONG FRIENDS

*"Friendship is held to be the severest
test of character. It is easy, we think,
to be loyal to a family and clan,
whose blood is in your own veins."*

Charles Eastman

Dakota Flat High School in BigTon, Colorado begins the school year with the sweltering days of summer not yet faded from the horizon. A warm morning breeze does little to encourage the lingering thermal waves. Signs of the day's humidity are drifting in from a mountain stronghold. The fading days of August signal a flurry of activity during pre-registration at the school. Incoming freshman and transfer students are to attend orientation a week before the first day of class.

Dacia and Pamela are involved in an early morning discussion concerning appropriate school wardrobe.

"Why can't I just wear my favorite dark green skirt? It looks cool with the light orange sweater that we bought last week. I do not understand why you have to check out every, single thing that I wear. You just do not trust me. You think that I cannot make good decisions. You know, mom, I am not a little kid. I know what to wear."

Dacia is indignant with her statement that she spouts off as she glamorously admires herself in the full-length, bedroom mirror, trying to avoid her mother's scornful glance.

"Since when have you been so concerned about what you wear? Just this past weekend I could not get you out of your dirty jeans and torn tee shirt. Do you remember the discussion we had when I wanted to fix your hair for the last Chamber of Commerce dinner? You told me that I was pulling your hair out when I tried to curl it for you."

Pamela retorts as she walks, uninvited, into her daughter's room. "That nice blouse with the small flowers on it that we bought at the specialty shop goes nicely with your new slacks. You look very 'nice' in that outfit."

"Oh mom," Dacia says with a sigh of exasperation, "no one says things like that anymore. Things like 'nice' and 'little flowers' aren't what kids want to hear these days. Besides, it has been a long time since your freshman days in high school. What do you know about teenage fashion?"

Dacia speaks as she continues to examine her pleasing reflection without really expecting a reply. It is more of a rhetorical question.

"I don't want to be rude, mom. I just feel so excited, scared, and confused all at the same time. It is as though I am a premiere ballerina who is performing for a prominent royal personality and my feet are tangled, cooked spaghetti. I just know that one of my new teachers is going to ask me a question when I'm in front of the class, and I won't know the answer."

Dacia is speaking in a voice which her mother has not often heard coming from her daughter. Her demeanor changes quickly. She is now a scared little girl instead of the confident, somewhat cocky teenager that her mother had seen just moments before.

"Sweetie, you are beautiful, smart, and well-informed. That is everything you need for this day. You will meet some new friends that may be with you for the rest of your life. Besides, you looked at the subjects, and elementary science is on your list. You love that subject. Just get in to meet your homeroom teacher, and you will feel more at ease. You will be fine."

Pamela feels her words 'falling on deaf ears' as she speaks them. Even her voice, which is faltering, almost betrays her. She remembers her first day as a freshman in high school; everything is scary, chaotic, and possible.

"Dacia, I'll drive you to school but don't worry, I won't kiss you goodbye in front of all the kids. But we need to hurry."

Pamela says with a tone of urgency while remembering her embarrassment at 'having parents' when she's a teenage girl.

As the car drives up to the building, Dacia is impressed. The sheer size of the Dakota Flats High School campus is overwhelming. It's her orientation week, but she is already feeling small and insignificant. She, however, can "handle" this situation. If surviving and growing within her family is any indication of her potential, Dacia certainly can work within this system. She quickly gets out of the front seat of Pamela's car and shuts the door as though she has no concern for the vehicle. Pamela rolls down the window to wish her daughter a successful orientation and to voice a greeting of affection.

"Dacia, enjoy the day. I'll be back to pick you up when school is out."

Dacia is already half-way up the sidewalk and turns only partially toward her mother's voice. With a wave of her hand, Dacia motions for her mother to drive away with a hesitant acknowledgment of relationship.

The high school hallway fills with anxious, hormone-surging, gawky teenagers looking for their homeroom and class syllabus. The scene resembles the nest of a great bird filling with newly hatching chicks all chirping, squawking and vying for that partially digested nourishment delivered by its parent. As in all cases, the entity that generates the greatest noise and physical energy get the quickest attention. Therefore, the chief education counselor is greeting the incoming students. She is filtering through the maze with a perception for a need that comes only with experience and urban knowledge of the inner workings of the adolescent mind.

Her name is Ms. McKim-DePue. Her years of experience brings her full circle in her career. She is now working with the children of the original students she met during her first year as a school advisor. Most of the kids call her 'Stinky Poo.' Not because she is awful but because she knows all of their secrets and swindles. You will be' hard pressed' to 'pull-one-over' on 'Stinky Poo.'

"Can I help you find something, Miss?" Hearing the words echo down the hallway, everyone freezes in place. No one answers the request. Again, the beacon rings out. "Can I help you find something, Miss?" The words are grating against the walls and removing pieces of plaster as they bounce.

Dacia, glancing up bewildered, sees that everyone in the hallway is staring in her direction, including Ms. McKim-DePue. She feels as if she is a sheet of paper in a room full of scissors. Dacia knows that her flaming-red hair is the beacon that captures the counselor's attention. It only takes a split second for Dacia's decision-making skills to kick in.

"I'm a freshman, here for orientation and need my class schedule. I also need some help with my locker."

Immediately, she realizes that the attention of the entire school balances on her. Everyone knows that you just never, under any circumstances, ask 'Stinky Poo' for help, especially not on the first day of school. She will have your name and know your face for the rest of your high school career. Already, Dacia realizes that she needs to fine-tune her skills. She knows that she must walk the gauntlet of the high school hallway toward 'Stinky Poo' to resolve her needs. There is no escape.

"Come here, Miss. I can help you find your class and show you a diagram of the school."

Dacia, knowing that there is no other option, begrudgingly walks over to the expressive counselor and presents her admission papers.

Having completed her first day of orientation, Dove is just leaving the school as the freshman are coming in for their initial introduction. She immediately focuses on the interaction between Ms. McKim-DePue and the tall girl with the fiery red hair. Dove is determined to make her quick exit so that the counselor does not focus on her, just to make sure that she does not need any assistance. She does not need the extra attention or frustration. However, the freshman sparks Dove-Whispering's interest, and she makes a note to introduce herself to the girl when regular classes begin.

"I'll walk you to your homeroom. I see that you have elementary science first on your list. I'll also take you to see our science teacher, Ms. Walters."

'Stinky Poo' talks excessively to Dacia and absently mindedly waves her hands as they walk through the winding halls of the school. Their sojourn ends with a meeting in the science lab with Ms. Walters, where the counselor makes her departure with a parting note,

"Dacia, I'll be here to help if you need assistance later with your classes. I know who you are and I certainly won't forget that beautiful fiery red hair." Dacia can find no place to hide, and she knows it. She thanks, Ms. McKim-DePue for her help.

"Well, hello. May I see your schedule for this year?" Ms. Walters, the science teacher says as she reaches out her hand in a friendly manner.

"You know, the transfer students were in here this morning. We talked a little about the classroom procedures for this year. It looks like we will have a good time learning about science. This class is the entry level for advanced programs. We are trying a new system this year, and it will be a combined class of freshmen and sophomore students. We are scheduling to do some projects together."

Dacia looks at the pile of the class syllabus on the table. She cannot wait to get home and read the list of topics. She also wants to make a good impression on the science teacher, so she is on her best behavior. However, her excitement is bubbling to the surface about the opportunity of entering the science class.

"I'm new to the school, but I want to make sure that my classes include the science class since I'm interested in the subject. I find that I am more involved in it than most of my other studies. When I read, which I do a lot, I like to pick out books on that subject."

She realizes that she is not breathing and stops abruptly in her speaking to take a deep breath. The fresh air fills her empty lungs. She guesses that it must feel like blowing breath into a flat balloon. Instantly, the bladder fills, and the air makes everything lighter, which is just how she feels after she takes her deep breath.

"Well, Dacia, don't worry. You are in this class. The class is a combination of sophomore transfer students, who need the class, and incoming freshmen. We will be looking at basic science issues at the beginning of the year. Then after the holiday break, the students will be 'pairing-up' and develop a science project. It is a regional contest.

The winners will then compete in the state competition. It sounds like you are interested in the project."

Ms. Walters stops her explanation and waits for Dacia's reaction.

"I have to check out my other classes, but this will be my favorite." Dacia takes the syllabus, shakes Ms. Walters hand and rushes out of the classroom, hoping that she does not meet 'Stinky Poo' on the way out. Dacia completes the school day and waits at the front door for her mom. She is excited to tell her about meeting Ms. Walters, the science teacher, and the strange, 'Stinky Poo.'

Dacia jumps into Pamela's car as soon as it pulls up.

"Guess who I saw today, Mom. There is Ms. Walters who I like a lot and an odd person who is known as 'Stinky Poo,' but her real name is Ms. McKim-DePue."

"Oh my, did you meet 'Stinky Poo'? I cannot believe that she is still around the place. I remember her from my high school days. She knows everything about all of the students. Once she identifies you, she follows and knows everything." Pamela tries not to alarm Dacia, but just the mention of the counselor's name brings back memories.

Pamela's high school memories begin fluctuating between her freshman and senior years. However, every incident, in some way, includes the intrusion of 'Stinky Poo.' Surely, 'Stinky Poo' cannot know that Dacia is her daughter. The counselor is simply focusing on a student who stands out in the crowd, for whatever reason. Pamela guesses that it is Dacia's cautious demeanor and flaming red hair that caught 'Stinky Poo's' attention.

In any regard, Pamela dismisses the encounter as a simple coincidence. The two females spend the ride home talking about Dacia's first experience at high school.

≈≈ ≈≈

Michelle and Dove-Whispering are discussing the day as well. The conversation intermingles with comments about meal preparation. The kitchen is small, causing each of them to squeeze past each other trying to complete different parts of their meal. Michelle finally asks,

"Dove-Whispering, you don't talk much about your day at school. I know that you are excited about it. Leaving Las Vegas was hard, sweetie. I hope that you will settle in okay."

Dove-Whispering is uncomfortable sharing her thoughts, even with her mother. She knows what her mom is looking for in her probing question. Michelle wants to know how she feels about her experience. Emotions, the area where Dove-Whispering feels most guarded.

Avoiding eye contact, she sighs and answers,

"It's good, I guess. Kids here act just as they do at the other school. Everyone is running to class, meeting teachers, and checking their schedules. The kids dress differently than in Las Vegas. Everyone here wears some boots. The counselor says that no one can wear shirts that are suggestive, whatever that means. Some kids cannot get into their lockers, but mine is fine. It is confusing because they have us transfer students coming in on the same day as the freshmen. Those people do not know anything about high school. It just causes a lot of mix up.

The counselors are in the hallway, but the teachers stay in their classrooms. I guess the kids are easier to see as they walk down the hallway. There is a weird looking counselor, she stands on the side of the front hallway and just looks at everybody. It is creepy. When she spots somebody having trouble or looking frustrated, she yells. They said that she has a weird nickname, but I don't know her name."

Michelle pushes her chair back from the kitchen table and walks over next to Dove-Whispering, softly placing her hands on her daughter's shoulders.

Speaking with parental concern, "I know that leaving Las Vegas was hard for you. You left friends in that town. Growing up with a close-knit family is good for you, and it is very hard to leave them. It gives you the ability to connect with your grandpa. He was in the delivery room when you were born. He truly loved you.

Grandpa was not around for us when we were young children. He worked out-of-town which meant that he traveled a lot. The last year before he died, he was sick and could not do things with you, but he loved you very much, Dove-Whispering. Everyone else called him William, but to you, he was always just grandpa.

It takes time to 'settle in' when you move to a new place, but we will do fine. Just give it time, sweetie."

"I know, mom. It is just like any other school. I did meet the science teacher, Ms. Walters. She mentions a science project that the transfer and freshman students will work on together. I like science. I might do it."

Dove-Whispering responds with covert indifference, so her mother will not detect her interest in the school science project. Whenever Michelle notes that her daughter is interested in a certain project, she becomes interested in that project as well. She wants to know every aspect and all the details. It is not because she is a nosy mother but because she dearly loves her daughter and wants to be part of the things that are of interest to her. Dove-Whispering learned this early in life and admittedly used this to manipulate her mother's interest to her advantage when needed. This time, however, Dove-Whispering just wants to have an interest and enjoy the project. She does not want help, assistance, or guidance from her mom. Dove-Whispering just wants to have a school project and see the results. She decides to keep the details of the science project to herself until she learns more information from the teacher, Ms. Walters.

"Well, sweetie, if you need any help, I am always available. I have great ideas since my interest in science earned me the position as the lead science instructor at my school. I also have great project ideas."

Michelle tries to conceal her excitement even though this may provide an opportunity to spend quality time with her daughter. Dove-Whispering is growing up quickly, and Michelle knows that her daughter will soon be in college. When that happens, she will enter the new world of young adulthood, and they may grow apart both physically and psychologically. Michelle wants to spend all the time she can with her child before that big change begins.

"Yeah, mom. Okay, we'll see." Dove-Whispering responds with vague commitment.

Dove-Whispering spends the remainder of the day reviewing her wardrobe, trying to decide on just the right outfit for the first full week of school. She notices that boots seem to be the popular footwear at Dakota Flats High School. The shoe section of her closet contains flats, sandals, and flip-flops. She will need some new shoes.

Her Auntie Anne is always good for a shopping trip to the shoe store. She instantly thinks of her aunt and uncle living in Las Vegas and misses them, terribly. Sadness spreads through her heart as though someone is shooting a syringe filled with memories into the soft tissue of her inner body. She feels soft and vulnerable inside. Her tears start. She closes the closet door, always embarrassed when showing emotions - it makes her feel fragile. She slumps to the floor, with darkness accepting her, and finally enjoys a great, cleansing, flooding, cathartic cry.

Dacia lines up all of her favorite boots. She wants to pick just the right ones for her first week at school. She can wear her special hiking ones or the comfortable pair with the little red hearts on the side, but those do not seem just right. She decides on the dark brown pair that was a birthday gift from her mom. Her closet seems full of children's clothes and summer outfits. She is looking for combinations that she can intermix to make five outfits for the entire week. Locating a couple of jeans and her favorite skirt is easy, but no tops seemed to match. It is work to dress like a high school student.

Her closet is located toward the back of the apartment, but she hears the muffled ring of the doorbell. Listening closely, she hears the sound repeat. She also hears her mother talking to someone at the apartment's front door.

She recognizes the voice as Mr. Menendez. He does not stop by their house often in the evening, so he must want to discuss something important.

She listens carefully but can only hear a muffled conversation of Mr. Menendez and her mother coming from the kitchen area. There is also the intermittent light clink of her mom's fine china cups. Is Pamela serving on her "company" china? We use the special dinnerware for a special visit.

What surprises her the most is that Mr. Menendez comes to the house as a guest? He is part of their family and has been since before Dacia's birth. Her mom relates stories of William and Mr. Menendez working together in the insurance business even before she and William met each other. Why was Mr. Menendez coming to their house at night in such a secretive, formal fashion? Dacia goes up to the front room and listens quietly at the edge of the kitchen door.

"Well, Mr. Menendez, what brings you here this evening? Is it something about chamber business? I think that the health fair is a great aide for the community. You do remember what important information I discovered at the last health fair?"

Pamela refers to her pregnancy test while shyly looking into her guest's inquisitive eyes, waiting for an answer already known. Both of the occupants sit at the kitchen table sharply remembering the day Pamela took the test at the health fair, discovering her pregnancy. Silence fills the room as if earplugs blocked every broadcasting network in the world, deafening and telling.

Mr. Menendez appears uncomfortable, fidgeting with his tie and clearing his throat with a gruff cough, breaking the silence.

"Pamela, I need to tell you something I have known about for a long time. This information is important, so I want to talk in confidence. Where is Dacia? You may not want her to hear this right now. You can decide for yourself after you listen to what I have to say." The nighttime guest adjusts his chair closer to Pamela as if he were a bumblebee hovering for just the right nectar to take back to his hive.

"Mr. Menendez, what is so important that you come to my house at night under an air of covert suspicion? You have my total attention." Pamela states with a slight hint of fear. She senses that her lifelong friend feels inadequate - an emotion that Mr. Menendez has never professed. He is an adopted father figure for Pamela, a strong, stable, secure man of good heart. It makes her nervous to discover that this pillar of stability may have a weak spot.

"Before I say anything, Pamela, you must understand that I love you as my daughter. I feel as if Dacia is my grandchild. Knowing you since birth is the bond between us. Your parents asked me to watch and protect you; they asked me before they died. I take the pledge seriously and still hold it dear to my heart." Mr. Menendez stops talking–being overwhelmed by emotion. He takes a sip of water from the glass that Pamela has absent-mindedly provided.

"My information concerns William. I know that you want to develop a life with him. Your feelings are strong. You may even truly love him. Dacia sees him as a father. It has been almost two years since you have seen him on a steady schedule. You mention that he is calling, but I know that you haven't had a conversation with him lately."

Mr. Menendez stops again in his litany. His breathing quickens now, his right foot is tapping the floor in a rhythmic, nervous pattern, and he looks like a hovering bee. Pamela can see that he is uncomfortable. She pulls her chair close beside him as if to say 'it's alright, you can tell me.' Mr. Menendez breathes deeply and continues:

"William is married. I knew this before I hired him. He would spend a lot of time away from his family if he took the job and William did not seem to be concerned. I never anticipated that William would start a relationship with you. I am responsible for this whole mess; I will tell you the whole story. William is married to a woman in Nevada for over thirty years. He also has three children who respect him as a father. I have been to Nevada and met his family.

It is a loving group but has little knowledge of William's other activities. He had other girlfriends. It surprised him when he learned that you were going to have his child. It is the first time that William is in a relationship that has trapped him. He just could not get out of it. I am not saying that to be rude or cruel to you but to let you know that William was not an upstanding character. William liked to play around but did not want to take on the responsibility.

I talk to you now about William in the past tense because, Pamela, he died. Remember when I took a long trip to Nevada a few months ago. Well, it was not for business. It was to pay a visit to William. He went back to his home in Nevada to visit his private doctor because he discovered a large bulge in his lower abdomen. The presence of it shook him. His doctor diagnosed cancer and William started on chemotherapy. Things did not go well from there. He is admitted to hospice on home care. Pamela, he is gone.

I cannot imagine a worse situation. My wife and I discuss the options often. She encouraged me to step-in as your relationship developed. I talked with him and tried to convince him that he should back off from you. He refused, saying, 'It's my business if I want to have a girlfriend.'"

Mr. Menendez clenches over in a defeated position focusing on his recitation and does not notice Pamela's reaction to his eulogy of her life. She sits quietly at the table facing Mr. Menendez, studying his face while listening to every word flowing from his mouth. She finds herself breathing deeply in unison with Mr. Menendez. Minutes pass before Pamela realizes she cannot convince her body to move. It is as if an ice storm has coated the two stationary bodies with layers of crystallized blankets and they freeze in place.

Mr. Menendez brakes the mood with his apologetic statement, "I'm so very sorry that I let this whole situation happen, Pamela. Bringing William into our lives was my mistake. Meeting him in Nevada seemed to be a good option for me. I was looking to expand the company, and he was eager to travel. He stated that he wanted to make money for his family. I believed that he would help me build the business and then send his profits back to his family. That was our plan. My mistake was in not knowing William. He was not what he appeared to be. There was always a 'story' of some kind from him. Believing in his version of a wide-eyed future was my mistake."

Mr. Menendez could sense the bitterness and heartbreak building in Pamela with each spoken word. His words are falling into a deep, bottomless well, being gobbled up by a cold, dark cauldron.

"Are you telling me that William never intended to, and wasn't legally able to, marry me? That is not possible. We love each other. Whenever he travels, there is always time in his schedule to call me and profess his love. I do not understand why he would keep talking to me about our lives together if he knew that we would never have such a thing. You are lying to me. You are lying to me. Why would you tell me such a horrible lie?"

Pamela rises from her chair with such force that it crashes up against the cabinet. The sound echoes through the apartment like a bullet discharging from a pistol. Dacia, who is trying to hide, instantly jumps and rushes to the kitchen, fearing she may find her mother injured on the floor.

Dacia catches her breath and struggles to respond to the disruptive scene she finds in the kitchen. "Mom, what happened? Are you hurt? Did you fall? Mr. Menendez, what did you do?" Dacia's voice reflects her concern and confusion in that her words sound as if they are coming from the mouth of an animated puppet. She stands in the kitchen doorway, frozen in place as she speaks.

Mr. Menendez realizes that he must control the situation since he does not want the scene to escalate. Before responding to Dacia, he makes a mental attempt to lower the tone of his voice and even-out his erratic emotions. His love for these two women is overwhelming for him, and the pain of disappointing those bores into his spiritual core. He breathes heavily, collects his emotions and begrudges himself for the reply he must give. "Your mom and I are talking about your dad. I am telling her some information that she did not know about his life. I am sure that she will talk to you when she feels a little better. She is just upset right now." He could not make eye contact with his adopted "granddaughter," Dacia. The protective feeling for her and Pamela cascades over him as though he is caught in a tsunami wave as it hits the beach.

Mr. Menendez let himself out of the apartment still carrying a heavy mental burden of untold truths concerning William. How could he have told Pamela that William's trips for business were just a cover story for the truth, he was making trips home to his family. Mr. Menendez always knew that William would never marry Pamela. She easily accepts a lie. He hates himself for lying to a person whom he considers a daughter. He scurries home to his wife feeling much like a large, river rat who has just stolen the fragile heart of a sweet, young thing under cover of darkness.

Dacia sits quietly next to her mother in the kitchen, carefully avoiding the seat previously occupied by their late night visitor. Both females are silent, while their minds analyze the scene they just experienced. Dacia can tell that her mother is upset even though she has heard only a muffled conversation coming from the kitchen before the crash, and there is little hint as to what Mr. Menendez told her mother. Pamela is on the verge of crying. Mother and daughter sit huddled in the dark kitchen, each pondering the next question. Numbness, pain, betrayal, humiliation, and despair all seem to be competing for a position in Pamela's head.

She repeats and repeats in her head, first softly and in a fit of rage – the same question she asks Mr. Menendez. "Why would William talk about our lives together if he knew that there could never be one?"

Pamela is first to speak, taking a deep sigh while adjusting her clothing. "Well, we sure did have an unexpected visitor tonight. Mr. Menendez came over to talk about some activities your dad did with the Chamber of Commerce." Pamela is not a good liar. "The information caught me off guard because I didn't expect that so many changes will be occurring so quickly," instantly deciding she could not let Dacia know the true reason for the late night visitor. Pamela's world shatters with one unexpected visitor. She and Dacia are a family of two now. Visits from William will not occur. Telling Dacia will take tact and deliberation, but it will not happen tonight, and it cannot happen tonight.

"Mom, you sure did react as though someone hit you. The chair smashed the cabinet, hard. I thought you were hurt. You get too emotional about things that might not matter. Mr. Menendez must worry too because he never comes here late at night. Why were you whispering in the kitchen? I couldn't hear what you said."

Dacia speaks while attempting to make eye contact with her mom. Pamela evades the gestures by repeatedly running her fingers over imaginary wrinkles on the top of her bathrobe. The two huddled figures remain somber and self-soothing, each frantically devising an internal mental strategy that will help to make sense out of an obvious senseless occurrence. Their closeness acts as a layer of healing balm that covers and calms the raw emotions, Pamela struggling to contain an explosive secret and Dacia searching to understand the covert message under the cloak of darkness. If a person did not know better, one would think that these two women are just having a late night chat at the kitchen table.

Dacia feels her mother's body slowly relax. It is only then that Dacia realizes that she is squeezing her mother's hands so tightly that her fingers are now an odd shade of purple. Instantly letting loose of her grip, allows Pamela to move her hands and circulate her fingers. Pamela slowly retreats to her bedroom. She cannot allow her daughter to observe the onslaught of tears about to occur. The flood will not wash away the stigmata inflicted upon the Henry family by a most devious and nefarious traveler, but it may begin the process of understanding and acceptance by family members who must endure the social and personal identity of that "branding." Devastation in the form of betrayal and dishonesty has changed their family. William is dead. Dacia is a bastard. Pamela is now, "the other woman."

⊨⊩ ⊪⊨

Only after Dacia is convinced that her mother is calm and safe does she return to her previous activity of picking out just the right outfit for school. It is an important endeavor since she will be entering high school tomorrow and a good first impression is important. She decides on the light brown boots since she wears them when she wants to feel special. Besides, making a good impression on the science teacher, Ms. Walters, is important to Dacia and she knows that Ms. Walters likes to wear boots.

Sleep is "hard won" that evening for Dacia. It is as though little birds are flying around in her head chirping about all the activities going on in Dacia's family. Finally, she falls asleep and envisions classrooms, special boots, science classes and meeting new friends.

Slumber comes easy for Dove-Whispering on the evening before the first day of her new school. Moving away from her "family home," dealing with the loss of her beloved grandpa, saying final "good-byes" to lifelong friends and adjusting to another new school, is exhausting. However, she does look forward to a new friendship, and she senses that her quick glance at the girl in the school hallway with the long, flaming, red hair will turn into a friendship. Dove-Whispering, she is Dove at school, feels as though she knows the girl already, yet is certain that they have never met. Maybe, that is how it feels when you are about to meet a lifelong friend?

CHAPTER 10

THE MOTHERS

"The more a daughter knows the details of her mother's life...the stronger the daughter."

Anita Diamant, *The Red Tent*

Kaye finishes her telephone conversation with her daughter, Michelle. It is time for a short visit to Colorado. Kaye is anxious to see her granddaughter, Dove-Whispering and Michelle will enjoy the company. Possibly, Auntie Anne will want to visit also. She is feeling better and recovering well from her surgery, having received Michelle's kidney just a few years ago. Michelle tolerates the cross-country trip during her recent move to Colorado, and her normal energy is returning. The assistance during her relocation of her older brother, Benedict, certainly makes the entire experience less hectic. This visit will be a good reunion opportunity for the "Henry" girls – mother, daughters, and granddaughter.

The trip from Nevada to Colorado will take some planning. Kaye needs to schedule around her work at the clinic. Anne is hard pressed to arrange her time off at the culinary office and Michelle, and Dove-Whispering need to check their school calendars. The past year has been more of a recovery period than of a mark of time. The Henry family children make a concerted effort to stay in touch and celebrate holidays due largely to the assistance of their mother, Kaye. Each family member is still dealing with the emotionally ravaged trash left in their lives by their father. Although the memories of interactions with their dad are warm and tender, they realize that what they experienced is not the true basis of their father's character. They each experience periods of crying and screaming, and cussing, and yelling at not only each other but also the world, when they realize that their father chose to live life in relationships with women in addition to their mother. The realization of its crushing blow threatens to tear at the basic fabric of their family unit.

However, digging deep into the essence of their family unit, they make an effort to stay close to each other as they work through the grieving process and the grief of losing their "idea" of the perfect dad. The children, Michelle, Anne, and Benedict, form a bond so strong it resembles the fibers of a polymer cable whose strength increases when stretched. In the process, each has grown into the early throngs of adulthood and can take a more realistic view of not only their father but also human relationships in general. Even though the siblings achieve adulthood, their emotional efforts remain in flux.

Kaye starts planning the trip. She can arrange a two-week period off from her position at the clinic. Time off from work has been scarce lately. The last time that Kaye took time off from work was to arrange William's funeral. Just the painful thought of that time still brings sadness to Kaye even though it has been a few years since the emotional event.

Taking a pause in her busy schedule, she reflects on the progress in her children since that time. Each has grown in their way while attempting to understand and deal with the realization of their father's lifestyle. She sees that they have adopted a broader sense of the world, yet are still struggling with the ideas of commitment and honesty in relationships. Her son, Benedict, seems to be struggling more than Anne or Michelle. That may be because his son-to-father relationship with William was such a tight bond. It is hard to know.

A phone call interrupts her thoughts. Much like a bird who quickly plucks the brightest red cherry right from the middle of a cluster of equally bulging fruits. It disturbs the tranquil scene. Kaye patiently listens as Michelle exclaimed her excitement about the upcoming trip. She is excited about her mother and sister visiting she and her daughter, Dove-Whispering in Colorado. They settled into their apartment and knew the surrounding area well enough to take their visitors on a historically accurate tour of the area. Michelle also relates to her mother that Dove-Whispering's new high school scheduled a parent-teacher night and they can all attend the function during their stay. It will be a good opportunity for everyone to tour the high school and meet Dove-Whispering's new teachers and classmates.

Kaye is taking the family photo album so that everyone can look at the collection of pictures. This variety of photos traces the lives of their family since before the children were born. The pictures include snapshots of William and Kaye as young adults enjoying life as they develop their relationship. Although it is obvious that Kaye removed most of William's pictures, she still remembers that rage-filled day when she tore through the album trying to obliterate evidence of her unfaithful husband from the family structure. There are a few pictures of "pa-pa" left in obscure places. The most recent snapshots are school pictures of Dove-Whispering as she poses for her sophomore school pictures. This cycle encompasses fifty years of activities of the Henry family life. The portraits include Dove-Whispering's great-grandmother, grandmother, mother, and auntie, all women who offer the young teen examples of female perseverance, determination, intelligence, and tenacity, the very soul of their family unit. It is a large, heavy book but will fit easily into the storage unit of the car.

Anne and Kaye decide to drive from Nevada to Colorado during the first couple days of their vacation. Both can schedule a few days off from their jobs and are grateful to have some time together while making the two-day drive. Benedict, Kaye's son, isn't able to make the trip but offers to map out the cross country drive that he took when moving Michelle and Dove-Whispering from Nevada to Colorado. It's a great help since he has marked the gas stops and safe rest areas.

"Mom, don't forget to pack that new medical book that we bought for Dove-Whispering. She will want to see it as soon as we get to their house. I talked with her yesterday, and she is excited about our trip. She likes her new school and is interested in the science class."

Anne is so excited about the upcoming trip that she is practically yelling from her bedroom as she packs for the trip, the tone of her voice can't hide her feelings. She doesn't care because seeing her favorite niece is the most exciting adventure that she has had in the last year.

"I know, Anne; I put it in the car already. It's big and bulky, so I wanted to make sure that we have room. It fits nicely in the back. We can finish packing and start driving in the morning. Our drive to Colorado will probably take about twelve hours. Benedict mapped out a good route. It's the one that he and Michelle took when they first drove out there."

Kaye is also excited about the trip. Even though Michelle and Benedict both tell her that the apartment in Colorado is in a safe part of town, she just wants to see for herself. Sometimes a mother just has to see things first hand.

Anne and Kaye follow Benedict's route, checking in with Michelle periodically during the trip. During one of Dove-Whispering talks on the phone, she reminds Kaye of a standing family joke. "Whenever we all have a get-together, grandma, I have too many mothers. Auntie is like my mom, you do things like my mom, and then I always have my real mom around. It's like having a house full of moms. I get confused and have too many things to do."

Kaye smiles because she understands what Dove-Whispering is saying - too many moms. Since Dove-Whispering is the youngest female in the group, she is the receiver of all of the female advice, all of the tried-and-true wisdom of the world. Kaye always answers the same way when the subject of moms comes into the conversation.

"I know Dove-Whispering, moms can be irritating some-times but just think of all the support and free advice that you have at your fingertips, we all love you dearly, and you never know when you may need the support of a circle of strong, intelligent women. Besides, when things get too "big" for you, you can always call up Uncle Benedict and spend some time with him."

"I know, grandma, and I love everybody, but I just want to say that sometimes it's a lot." Dove-Whispering was try-ing to let grandma know that she loved her but didn't want her in her teenaged world all the time.

As they ended the phone call, Kaye also wanted her precious granddaughter to know that she did understand about not invading her precious teenage girl privacy.

"Sweetie, I understand about getting into your space. Remember, I was a girl once myself. All of your mothers can be a little much, I agree. We love you so much. It's hard sometimes for us not to give you advice. We are try-ing, and I think that we are getting better at not being in your face. We will get better." Kaye said goodbye to her granddaughter and sent her a kiss by phone.

Kaye talks with Anne about the phone conversation with Dove-Whispering. Anne agrees that often her niece does have "too many moms," Anne delicately approaches the subject.

"Mom, we all do get into Dove-Whispering's business. Whenever she has a test at school or is going to a special function, we are all excited and try to plan out every detail. It's not because we want to be in charge but because we love her so much and want only the best for her. We have our ideas and want things done a certain way. This view usually causes confusion. Dove-Whispering has been able to deal with our way of doing things. However, she is now a young woman, and she is also strong and independent. She will be herself. She loves us but will pick her road."

Anne is standing by the car, which is finally packed for their Colorado trip, as she relates her feelings about her niece. Kaye listens intently, knowing that her youngest daughter is her child with the "ole'soul" and can understand people.

Kaye responds, "You are right, Anne. I notice that Dove-Whispering quietly listens to people before she responds. It is as if you can hear her brain "thinking." She thinks before she speaks. Some interpret this as shyness, but it is just Dove-Whispering deciding how she will respond. However, once she makes a decision, she is dedicated to that goal. She is certainly like the rest of us in that respect." Kaye and Anne agree that the visit to Colorado will certainly be interesting.

Just as Kaye and Anne are crossing the state line between Utah and Colorado, Kaye receives a cell phone call from Michelle, Dove-Whispering's mother. "Mom, I'm so excited that you guys are coming for a visit. We have so much scheduled while you're here. There's a parent-teacher conference at Dove-Whispering's new high school, and she wants us all to come. We also can take a tour of the science center at my school also. There is a new history center opening in Denver that I have wanted to see. We can all go there too."

Michelle is talking so fast that Kaye can't get Michelle to pause long enough to answer questions. Kaye interrupts the conversation: "Michelle, I know that you are excited about us coming but just take a breath. We aren't even there yet. We want to spend time with you and Dove-Whispering. Don't feel like you need to entertain us. We will be comfortable just spending time at home, being with you."

There is a moment of silence on the other end of the phone line. "You're right, mom. My schedule is so busy with my work and Dove-Whispering's school schedule that I focus toward trying to pack just one more activity into our day. Your visit will be a time for us to take a well-needed break. I just want to make sure that you and Anne have a safe trip. Will you call me as you drive and let me know how the drive is going?"

"Of course, sweetie. We'll let you know when we get gas and use the rest stops that Benedict mapped for our trip. We'll be fine." Kaye knew that Michelle would worry until she saw them pull up in the driveway at her home in Colorado.

"There is just one function that Dove-Whispering wants us to do. It is the parent-teacher conference at her high school. She is settling in and likes most of her classes. Her favorite is the science class. The teacher, Ms. Walters seems to be able to get the kids involved in the class. Also, there is a new friend that Dove-Whispering has been discussing. She met her at school, and they sit next to each other in the science class. Oh well, mom, we can talk about all of this when you guys get here. Be safe. See ya soon." Kaye takes a deep breath as she hangs up the phone.

Anne couldn't help but overhear Kaye's phone conversation. "It sounds like we will be busy in Colorado. We always have a good time when we get together, and I know that we will be just fine. There are usually more activities planned than we can do."

"I agree, Anne. I am already tired but glad that we will spend time together," Kaye noted that they were crossing over the Colorado state line as she was speaking. She reflected on the personalities of her three children. Benedict was stoic, yet sometimes over-protective, Anne was her soft-hearted, caring soul and Michelle was her sanguine child who was always good at planning and organizing. The three made a perfect triad of children for the busy Henry family.

Arriving in BigTon, Colorado causes quite a stir in Michelle's household. Everyone is excited to greet the guests. Dove-Whispering greets her grandmother and aunt at the front door.

"Hi, you guys. We have been waiting for you. How was the trip? Boy, have we got something to show you. There is something special in our house now. It is a new addition, a dog. Her name is Kiko, and I love her so much. She looks just like that famous dog in Japan who always waited for her master to come home from work on the train. The dog would wait outside of the train station and watch everyone until he spotted his master and then they would walk home together. Oh, grandma, I love Kiko so much. Come on in and meet her."

Anne and Kaye enter Michelle's apartment amid a flurry of activity, barely squeezing through the doorway. It seems as though they are freshly made dough forming into noodles readied for a prized pasta dish. They put down their baggage and steady themselves against the onslaught of puppy playfulness. Dove-Whispering can hardly contain her excitement thinking of the upcoming activities with her family. It isn't often that her mother, auntie, and grandmother are together and ready to be with her for a whole week. She is especially looking forward to the parent-teacher conference at her new high school.

Her excitement overcomes her and interrupts the adult conversation, "I want to make sure that we get to the school early so that there's time to see all of my teachers, especially the science teacher, Ms. Walters. I like the class, and she is a good teacher."

"Take a breath, girl." Michelle interrupted. "They haven't even settled yet. Let them rest a bit tonight, and we can talk about our plans in the morning."

Dove-Whispering takes a deep breath, stiffens her body and immediately looks for a source in which she can stifle her excitement. She finds it by hugging the ample, furry neck of Kiko, who is always at her side. The youngest, usually pensive Henry female finds it difficult to reign in her emotions once they grabbed hold of her.

"Don't you worry my sweet child. We will certainly get all the things done that you want do. Auntie and I want to make this visit fun, and we will do all the good stuff for you." Dove-Whispering grandmother gently walked over to her granddaughter, mindful of the protective eye of her canine protector, and swoops her up in a loving embrace, encircling her body around her grandchild so completely that the two appear to melt into one person.

"Wait, I want to get in on this love fest, too." Auntie Anne rushes over and spreads her outstretched arms around the enmeshed forms while giving out a smacking sound from her lips that indicates she is sending kisses to the entwined group.

Sensing their emotions, Kiko gives out a low moan which slowly rises to a high-pitched howl, echoing the general sentiment of the huddled group. Michelle can contain her emotions, no longer. She emulates and repeats the primal howl, increasing the tone with each utterance. Soon, the entire huddle of Henry females is enjoying a good, ole' primal howl in the middle of the living room, in the middle of the evening it's a good thing. Little do they realize that this huddled closeness may be their last naïve refuge.

CHAPTER 11
PARENT-TEACHER NIGHT

*"The best teachers show you where to
look but don't tell you what to see."*

Alexandra K. Trenton

Ms. Mckim-Depue, known to the students as 'Stinky Poo,' assumes her normal position for formal functions such as these. She looks especially sharp in her molded, red-tinged beehive hairstyle and ornate black glasses edged with just a bit of sparkle on the tips. She considers changing her hairstyle, but her mother mentioned that women who become flirtatious with their hairdos attract the "wrong type of men." So, for now, she will keep her tried and true look and remain a respectable woman.

In her younger years, she sported a full head of carrot-red curly hair that shined and tangled in the warm morning

wind. It truly resembled a bunch of newly harvested veg-
etables ready for prominent display at the farmers market.
Over the years, she learns that it is more respectable to contain her assets into a proper style.

Memories of a by-gone day still physically walk in her everyday life as a constant reminder of her a youthful, romantic interlude. A prominent local family became the child's
parents. They owned a prosperous hotel for "well-heeled"
guests in BigTon, Colorado. Mr. Menendez, a leader in the
local Chamber of Commerce, was instrumental in securing
just the right prominent couple to adopt the child. Every
effort was made to ensure that the child never knew her
true parentage or of the adoption, and all involved swore
secrecy. Ms. McKim-Depue watched her daughter grow
from afar. She accepted a position as a librarian with the
elementary school system when Pamela was progressing
through the lower school system. When the girl reaches
her teenage years, Ms. Mckim-Depue secures a job as a high
school counselor to safely observe her child. She attends
her graduation ceremony and encourages the young woman whenever she observes her at Chamber of Commerce
functions.

Tonight especially, Ms. McKim-DePue anticipates the
attendance of her daughter, Pamela, and granddaughter,
Dacia, at the parent-teacher conferences. However, this
evening she is not a parent. She will not sit in the parent
section to learn of her child's progress within the school
system. She is not a family member.

Her duty this evening is to meet the high school parents
and students as they enter and direct them to the appropriate rooms. Everyone is on a tight schedule, and the routine

must go smoothly. She must not become emotional or falter in her duty to the students.

"Well, good evening, Dove, I see that you have some extra guests this evening. May I introduce myself? I am the school counselor, Ms. McKim-Depue. We have seen only a little of Dove this year, but we all expect great things from her." 'Stinky Poo' extends her hand toward Kaye and Anne as they enter following Dove and Michelle through the front door of the high school.

"We certainly are thrilled to be here. We traveled from Nevada. Dove is my granddaughter. My daughter, Michelle, and Dove just love the area and seem to be settling in very nicely. Dove is excited about this evening. She wants us to meet all of her teachers." Kaye speaks as she continues to shake Ms. McKim-Depue's hand. 'Stinky-Poo' holds the grip a little longer than is expected in a social setting. Kaye finally, politely pulls her hand away and quickly walks behind Anne.

"Yes, thank you. We are glad to be here." Anne takes the cue from her mom, nods toward Ms. McKim-DePue and follows the rest of the family into the gym for the information meeting.

Just as the Henry family is getting settled, Pamela and Dacia enter the front door of Dakota Flats High School. The counselor, Ms. McKim-DePue, pauses as she recognizes the adult woman accompanying the freshman student. The counselor notes that even though the child sports a head of bright red curly hair and the woman is adorned with long, beautiful straight, flowing blonde hair, the two females look strikingly similar.

The counselor approaches the woman. "Excuse me. But you look familiar to me. Have we seen each other before tonight?" Pamela catches her breath briefly before answering. Still feeling the intimidating sensation from her teenage years, she voices her answer: "Uh, Yes, Ms. McKim-DePue. You gave me a lot of trouble when I was a student in this school. I'm Pamela Love. You remember me because you were the counselor and I gave you a lot of trouble. I could never get away with anything. "

"Oh yes, Pamela, I do remember you. Yes, you surely did keep me on my toes. Well, I see that you did make it to adulthood. Dacia, your daughter, surely is like you in many ways, I guess." Ms. McKim-DePue says with a bit of sarcastic humor.

Pamela nods slightly, as much to end the conversation as to deny the statement. Dacia reaches for the program handed to her by the counselor but realizes that the counselor hasn't released her grip on the paper. For an awkward moment, both stand in the doorway holding opposite ends the program, each not quite sure what the next move should be. Ms. McKim-Depue stares at Dacia as though she wants to add something to their conversation, but she hesitates, and then reluctantly releases her grip on the paper. Pamela and Dacia thank her for the program and walk toward the orientation meeting in the school gym, unaware of the family history held by "the weird looking school counselor who everyone makes fun of in the hallway."

Pamela leans down and whispers to Dacia, " Somethings will never change."

As they enter the gym, Dacia spots Dove sitting with a few women that Dacia doesn't know. She guesses that they are Dove's family. Dacia wonders if Dove's father will be at the meeting tonight also. Dove never seems to talk about her dad. When the subject came up, it was as if a small bird constantly chirped for its missing parent.

The orientation meeting ends quickly, and the students and parents depart to their respective rooms to meet with their designated teachers. Even though the school has been in session for only a few weeks, Dove and Dacia develop a familiar relationship. Science is their bonding interest. Each likes the class and requests to sit in front row.

As parents complete their conference with a teacher, they move on to their next scheduled appointment with the next teacher. It seems that both Dacia and Dove have scheduled for Ms. Walters' science room at the same time. Therefore, they and their family's meet each other in the science lab.

Ms. Walters states the obvious: "What a coincidence. Scheduling like this doesn't usually happen that I have two students at the same time. It must be fate. Well, as long as everyone is here, we'll introduce you. Dacia and Dove already know each other. So let's see who else is here."

Michelle is the first to speak, "I'm Dove-Whispering's mother. Oh, excuse me. I'm Dove's mother. My name is Michelle. I'm excited that my daughter likes science because I'm the director of the science program at my school. I teach an elementary class in another part of town."

Kaye, who has been walking around the back of the room looking at the poster outlining the periodic table of elements, doesn't hesitate to introduce herself as Dove's grandmother. "We have driven from Nevada so that we can spend some time with our family. It's good that we can come here tonight to meet her teachers. My other daughter came with me."

Anne, who has been looking at the bunsen burners at the back of the room, chimes in – "I'm Dove's Auntie Anne and came to spend time with everyone for a while. I like the science room. When I was in school, it was always an interesting place for me. I know that Dove also like science."

Pamela and Dacia were standing in the doorway, listening to the introductions. Dacia, pulling her mother by the arm, brings Pamela over to the small cluster of people standing at the front of the science room. "I want everyone to meet my mother. Meet Pamela Love, my mom. Dove and I have been watching you, and we already know everyone."

Ms. Walters, realizing that the students have taken over the conference, interrupts the introductions. "Excuse me, Dacia. Thank you for completing the salutations for us. Now that we all know each other, maybe we can discuss some of the projects that we are working on this semester. I also would like to get to know both of you, Pamela and Michelle, so that we can foster a working relationship throughout the school year. I'm sure that the two girls will be excited about all of the upcoming events. Both of them have already shown a general interest in science."

Pamela speaks first: "I'm interested in having Dacia involved in any science projects early on in her school years. I was part of a project in my freshman and sophomore high school years here at Dakota Flats, and the program was chosen to compete in the regional competition finals. We learned a lot about the project itself, but also it gave us experience on how to work as a team and how to compare our project with other groups. I still remember the experience and the kids that I worked with on that assignment. Some of them became lifelong friends."

Michelle also voices an opinion: "I'm the science coordinator at my elementary school. Ms. Walters, if you need any help with research or supplies on projects throughout the year just let me know. I will be glad to help whenever I can. Dove has always been interested in outdoor projects and conservation ideas. I'm sure that she will be very helpful."

Ms. Walters eyes both Dacia and Dove as they fidget, these adult meetings seem filled with plans and ideas that decide things for kids. "Well, would you girls like to check out the science lab while I talk to your family?"

Dacia and Dove, happily take advantage of the release of the tether as they rush toward the science lab equipment. Ms. Walters continues: "We have plenty of supplies for our upcoming science competition. We usually present our projects in the spring, a month or so before the end of the school year. The winner of the school competition will compete in a regional program. If the regional winners place in the top two spaces of the competition, they will go to the state competition. The school has sent an entry to the state science competition level for the past few years. We are expecting to do the same this year. If Dacia and Dove are interested, they surely can work on a project together. An interest in science is basic, but an inquisitive mind is more important for a successful entry. I'll talk more about the project to both of them."

The school bell rang just as though it was a regular school day. However, it just announced the end of the parent-teacher conference. The sound startled the adults sending a jolt through their normal reserved stature, as though a fire truck was roaring down the school hallway.

Each student, of course, took the piercing note in stride since it was part of their everyday school routine, not a big deal.

"Well, it's time to leave. We surely have enjoyed meeting you, Ms. Walters, and seeing the science lab." Michelle states as she turns toward the science teacher from her position amid the bunsen burners and test tubes. "I want to make sure that we exchange contact phone number too, Ms. Love. We may want to stay in touch as the school year progresses. I have a feeling that our daughters will be involved with a science project."

"Of course, Ms. Henry, I would like to get to know you better also. We can talk on the phone and then meet for lunch." Pamela was talking as she wrote her phone number on a notepad that she removed from her pad and handed to Michelle.

Dacia and Dove walk arm-in-arm out of the science room half skipping down the school hallway. Ms. McKim-DePue meets them at the front door. Both girls stopped short in their gleeful stride. They note a faint smile on 'Stinky Poo's face, not an expected expression. "Well girls looks like you are having a good time this evening. I imagine that your teachers gave a good report to your parents."

Dacia urges Dove to speak first by nudging her in the back. "Yes, mam. It is just our moms here tonight, but everything went fine." Both girls are struggling to hold back a bursting giggle.

Ms. McKim-DePue's smile deepens as she stares into Dacia's eyes. The unexpected glance scares the girl, and Dacia quickly broke the gaze. "Come on Dove we came go out to the parking lot and wait for our moms at the car.

They won't be too long because the school is locked now." Dacia says with authority as both girls are already half-way out of the front door.

Dove follows Dacia out into the parking lot as she looks back and spies her mom and Ms. Love pausing briefly to talk with 'Stinky Poo' at the front door. "What do you think the women are talking about Dacia? Look they are standing at the door. They seem to be having a good time and laughing about something. Do you think that they are talking about us?" Dove says with a slight tinge of suspicion.

"Adults always talk about silly stuff when they meet new people. They try to make a good impression. My mom went to high school here, and she might know someone who also went here. They are probably talking about how things were in the ole' days. It's nothing. They'll finish soon." Dacia waves her hand in the air as she talks about the adults talking at the high school doorway as though she is dismissing an annoying gnat buzzing around her. However, she notices that Dove is getting concerned about the adult conversation.

"I don't know about that, Dacia. Sometimes, when adults meet other people, they get involved in other lives. They ask questions, especially women. I have seen my mother get to know other women, and then those women get to talking, and before you know it, we are having dinner with her family and getting to know all of the details of their family. Even the stuff that we don't want to know. We even get to know all of the family secrets that they don't tell anybody else. I hope that doesn't happen with our families. I just want to have you as a friend. I want us to be good buddies and enjoy taking science together and being in high school together. I don't want things to get messy. I just want to have a good friend, not another messy family; it's exhausting for everyone."

Dove is getting emotional as she continues to speak about family involvement and meeting new friends. Dacia walks over to her and tries to calm her fears and reassure that they will be friends, good friends. "We will be friends. Things will not get messy. Things will not be involved or drawn out into family stuff. We will just be two girls in high school who like science and do goofy things like any other kids. It will be fine. It will be good for us. Don't worry." Dacia stands next to Dove as they both lean against the cars in the high school parking lot as they look out toward the mountain range that rims the high school campus in BigTon, Colorado. They might well be a pair of Cocoon moths, secure in their hibernation but unaware of the flight path that they are about to enter.

CHAPTER 12
COMPARATIVE HISTORY

"The bottom line: if you want a happier family,
bring those skeletons out of the closet."

Bruce Feiler

"If you can't get rid of the family skeleton,
you may as well make it dance."

George Bernard Shaw

"Well, I have the best news. We are all going to have lunch together and get to know each other better. It will be in a week or so after Pam and Dacia check their schedules. I know that it will be great. We will have a lot of fun. Maybe we can also go to the local nature museum. I think that I have a couple of free passes." Michelle was bubbling with excitement as she and Anne return to the car. She and Anne were already planning the get-together as Michelle unlocked the car doors.

Dove-Whispering slowly opens the back door of the car and shakes her head because she was involved in this same situation before. Michelle is oblivious to her daughter's reluctant reaction to the upcoming social engagement. However, Anne silently watches her niece as Dove-Whispering sits quietly in the back seat. Anne knows her niece well enough to understand that when she becomes quiet, her thinking is intense about something. Dove-Whispering is trying to figure out how she feels about this situation since it bothers her. Dove-Whispering also senses that family relationships are about to get "messy," again. The meeting with Ms. Love and Dacia could lead to being intimately entwined into their lives, and Dove-Whispering did not want that to happen. As the Henry family approaches home, Anne decides to wait until later to discuss the subject with Dove-Whispering. However, the conversation quickly turns toward Dacia and Pamela.

"I noticed that Dacia's dad wasn't at the conference tonight, Dove-Whispering. Is there a reason for him not being there? I would like to meet him." Michelle says, driving away from the school in an off-handed manner as though she is inquiring about a new book arriving in the local library.

"I have never seen her dad," Dove-Whispering replies. "She doesn't talk about him at school, and I have never seen a picture of her family. I don't know if her dad is around or if he even lives with them." Dove-Whispering cringes as she answers her mom from the back seat and she can feel the tangled web of involvement beginning to grow between her family and Dacia's.

"Well, Dove-Whispering, I would like to know them a little better. We need some friends, and Pamela and Dacia seem like good people. If there are more members in her family, I would like to meet them. We have been in Colorado for such a short time, and I think that knowing more people will help us to settle into the area." Michelle continues driving oblivious to the effect that her words are having on Dove-Whispering. She feels as if someone is showering her with small grains of sand and she is buried up to her neck. Her mother always wants to get involved in her social affairs.

Kaye knows both her daughter and granddaughter very well. She senses that the conversation upsets her granddaughter. She also knows that her daughter is sanguine about affairs in general but does not want to offend or pressure her daughter. She feels compelled to offer her unsolicited opinion. "Michelle, maybe Mr. Henry wasn't there tonight because he was out of town on business or maybe he and Pamela are divorced. There could be any number of reasons for him not being at the school tonight. I am sure that those issues are not our business. If Dacia wants Dove-Whispering to know about her dad, there will be other opportunities."

"Well, I know mom, but our families seem to be so similar, like opposite sides of a mirror. Ms. Love is a single mom with a daughter, and that is like our family. Our families seem to be like peas in a pod, a single mom with a daughter. I was just wondering if that is truly the entire family. I wasn't trying to learn any personal information that is a secret." Michelle says with a slight note of forgiveness as she releases her right hand from the steering wheel and reaches across the back of the driver's seat toward her daughter in an attempt to soothe Dove-Whispering.

"It seems as though you and Dove-Whispering have settled in fairly well since your move. Dove-Whispering is making friends, and you like your job at the school. However, I do understand wanting to have a close-knit circle of friends." Kaye says with a grandmother's understanding tone.

Anne realizes that the conversation that she wants to delay until later with Dove-Whispering is playing out with her family members in the car right now. However, she still decides to wait until a time when the emotional environment is settled to have her conversation with her contemplative niece.

"Well, mom, I don't know stuff about their dad. I just know that I have a friend at school and we both like science. Ms. Walters says that we can work on the science project together even though we are in different grades. This year the freshmen and transfer students are in the same science class. We are deciding what our project will be for the competition. Maybe I will get to know her better as we work together." Dove-Whispering speaks with a tone of resignation as though she understands that her mother will eventually learn the full truth of the Henry family, her mother eventually learns the truth about everything.

"Everyone has had a very long day, we are tired and a little on edge. When we get a good night's rest, we will feel better. I, for one, will be glad to get into a nice warm bed and pull the covers over my head for a good sleep." Anne says sleepily as she 'cozies up' in the back seat next to her favorite niece.

"Auntie, I want to go to sleep, too. I am tired. I feel like I have to handle a lot of stuff, but I'm glad you're here." Dove-Whispering returns the favor and snuggles next to her auntie and yearns for a nice, warm blanket to cover them both as they huddle together, just like two blue birds shivering on a tree limb because they forgot to fly south for the winter. Dove-Whispering speaks in a barely audible whisper from under her covers, "Maybe everybody wonders where my dad was tonight," as she closes her large, almond-shaped, brown eyes.

Kaye states in her grandmotherly tone, "Well, I think that we want to know more about this Henry family just because they remind us of ourselves. Maybe if we find out more about them, we will find out more about ourselves. Is not that odd? There is a family like ours but lives in another state. A family that, for some reason, is intriguing to us. I wonder why we even care. Why do we want to know more about them? What draws us to this family? Why are Dacia and Dove-Whispering such good friends so quickly? Oh well, I guess that I feel like my granddaughter, sometimes I feel like I have to handle too much. I may be making too much out of all this. There may be no connection at all. It may be my imagination. I'm foolish."

Everyone else in the car answers in unison, "Yeah, Grandma, you always try to handle too much. You are making us all tired. When we get home, we're all going to bed."

≈≈+ +≈≈

"Meeting your new friend, Dove, this evening was nice, Dacia. She is beautiful. She also seems to like you a lot.

I noticed both of you huddling and whispering during the evening just like teenage girls do when they are good friends." Pamela says as she walks arm-in-arm with Dacia down the hallway toward the front door of the high school after attending the parent-teacher conference.

"Oh, mom. Do not hold my arm like that. We're in school, and I feel a little odd when we walk like that. Someone may see us and think that we are strange or something." Dacia states with a tone of embarrassment, quickly pulling her arm out of her mother's embrace.

"Yeah, she's a good kid. I like her okay I am glad that we like science. It is something that is not all tangled up with emotions and stuff. You only have to deal with facts and numbers. I didn't know if I would like high school, but we got together real quick." Dacia's voice softly trails off as she thinks of her first meeting with the transfer student, like fitting the last piece of a complicated puzzle into place.

Dacia's thoughts then briefly wonder to another emotional attachment in her life, her dad. His presence at the parent-teacher conference would have made this night complete. She remembers his captivating story-telling ability and the spellbinding web he wove when trying to convince someone of an idea. However, his presence in her life has disappeared. She is not sure where he went or if he will return, but her memories of him are still fresh and positive.

"Mom, we never had that talk about Dad. You avoid it. You keep saying that he is just working out-of-town on a long job. When I was younger, he would come and go. For the last year or so, he only calls, and we don't see him at all."

'Stinky-Poo' abruptly stops the couple at the front door. The school counselor approaches them with an air of inquisition and pride as though she was a family member inquiring about a holiday outing. "Well, good evening. How was the parent-teacher conference for you tonight? I saw that both of you spent a lot of time in the science room talking with Ms. Walters. I know that the school has a science competition each year. Are you going to work on that program, Dacia?" 'Stinky-Poo' steps in front of Dacia and Pamela so as to block their exit. Her intention is to initiate a brief, superficial conversation with the student that she has followed across her growing years. Even though the counselor has remained in the public background, the milestones of Pamela's life have not escaped attention.

"Uh, well, yes. I like science a lot. Ms. Walters wants us to pick a partner for the competition. Maybe, Dove-Whispering and I will work together." Dacia offers since she guessed that 'Stinky-Poo' would stand aside as soon as she got the intended information.

Pamela is less obliging and sympathetic. "Well, we talked to all of the teachers tonight. I guess that you were watching us too closely. Maybe you should not be so concerned about other's business?" Pamela makes sure that her direct eye contact delivers her message to the presumptive counselor.

'Stinky-Poo' quickly averts Pamela's eye contact and steps aside from the doorway. A pang of sorrow shoots through her heart like an arrow shot from Lucifer himself. Pamela is surprised at her response and walks outside questioning the reason for her quick and curt answer. The emotional response came from some unknown attachment inside. Pamela realizes that the counselor followed her all through her growing years and now is going to do the same to her daughter. It's like 'Stinky'Poo' is a fly that is always buzzing around your head bothering you and not doing anything productive, the counselor is always lurking in the background.

Dacia senses her mother's questioning attitude. "Mom, what's the matter with you? The counselor seems to have gotten to you. She has been around the school forever. Everyone knows that she isn't important. Why do you let her bother you? She is just a counselor."

"I know, dear, but she has been lurking around me ever since I was a little girl. She is unsettling. Seems like she also wants to know things about you too. It bothers me, that's all." Pamela walks arm-in-arm with Dacia toward their car, each in quiet thought. Their ride home is peppered with a superficial conversation about school, clothes and the upcoming science project.

The parent-teacher conference brought together two families that intertwine long before they met, William Henry, being their grounding point. They would all realize that their relationship encompassed secrets, skeletons, and betrayals that could affect future generations.

How could they know what lies ahead for them? Sisters and brothers would find new connections, aunts and nieces will unite, secret lovers revealed, and marriage partners betrayed. Long held truths disposed of and replaced by fragile alliances.

CHAPTER 13
THE INTRODUCTIONS

*"There is nothing more difficult to take in hand
more perilous to conduct or more uncertain
in it's success than to take the lead in the
introduction of a new order of things."*

Niccolo Machiavelli

*"It's much easier to get a reception from
someone if there is an introduction versus
randomly trying to get in front of people."*

Brad Feld

⊶ ⊷

Kaye is packing for the return trip to Nevada. Anne, Michelle, and Dove-Whispering are off visiting their long-time friends before the trip back home. To Dove-Whispering, the period before "saying good-bye" feels a little like a fledgling bird slowly pushed out of the familiar nest. She feels better when her family is close. However, she tends to keep her feelings to herself.

Michelle is driving everyone back from their last visit when she suggests that it might be a good idea to invite Dove-Whispering's new school friend over for dinner before Kaye and Anne return to Nevada. "We could ask Dacia and her mom, Pamela, over to our house this weekend before grandma and auntie leave. It would be a nice, intimate dinner where we could get to know everyone. Meeting them on a social level may be fun. We could get to know their family, and it may help Dacia and Dove-Whispering to form a friendship. It can be hard to meet friends when teenagers transfer into high school from another state."

This time Dove-Whispering speaks up with enthusiasm, "That would be great, Mom, I have wanted to know more about Dacia. She seems to know a lot about science. When I saw first saw her, I felt like I had met her before in my life. It was a strong feeling. Maybe we just have a lot in common. Yes, I would like to have them over for supper or something. It is a great idea. When can we do that?"

"Well, I think that we should do it pretty soon because we need to return to Nevada in a couple of days. So, maybe I can call Pamela tomorrow morning and invite them over for a day or two." Michelle wants her daughter to feel as though she is part of the school and community.

"That will be great." Dove-Whispering is delighted that her friendship with her school friend will now extend to her family. I hope that the two families will be able to share their backgrounds and become close, forever.

⊷ ⊶

"Pamela has accepted the invitation, and she and Dacia will be coming here for dinner tomorrow night. We can think about the menu. I'm not sure what they like to eat, but we'll make something that we like and see what happens." Michelle and Kaye are quick to look at Anne who is the culinary expert in their family. She is an excellent cook and can develop a menu quick that will please even the most discerning pallet.

"Oh Auntie, pick out something great. I want Mrs. Henry and Dacia to like us and like the menu too." Dove-Whispering can hardly contain her excitement at the prospect of having dinner guest, especially her best friend and her mother.

Anne is more than eager to start on the menu. She also wants some help and decides that Dove-Whispering will be just the right assistant. "Well, let's get started on the menu, my little niece. We need to have enough time to buy just the right ingredients and prepare the dishes in advance. Let's write out the menu first and then we can see which of us can best do each task."

Auntie Anne and Dove-Whispering busy themselves with dinner preparations. Michelle and Kaye make sure that the linens and family tablecloth are clean and ready for the dining room table. Pamela and Dacia are important guests. The china and linen are "family" treasures. They were her mother's and given to her when she moved to Colorado.

Kaye takes the family linen from the dining room bureau drawer. Her sensitive fingers trace the knobby cloth and firm threads of the heirloom material. Memories seem to bounce off from the small buds and infiltrate her mind. Her enjoyable memories involved family dinners when she,

William and their children gathered around the table enjoying festive holidays and sharing happy milestones in their lives. Laughter is easy, and smiles seem to float effortlessly. Life is busy, and the children are eager to share information about their everyday lives. William is sitting at the head of the table and Kaye is at the other end. She and William exchange glances as the meal progresses. The dinner conversation revolves around family small talk peppered with loving exchanges. Her mental retreat diverts as she reaches for the pieces of fine china positioned next to the linens in the bureau drawer. These plates, cups, saucers, and bowls are the mainstay of their heirloom dinners. Each holiday the festive table is set with "mom's" fine china. The plates positioned at each persons' designated place, then the accessories, salad bowl, dessert plate, water glass, fine silverware, bread dish and a linen napkin. The ritual is important. It is part of the holiday routine. The family expects the process. The linen tablecloth goes with the china, and the china goes with the fine silverware. The children feel special when they place the items on the table. They know the routine. That is the way it always was.

"Mom, have you seen the large cooking pot?" The solitude of Kaye's memory sequence instantly collides with Michelle's probing question. It takes a few moments for Kaye to realize that she is transformed back into Michelle's dining room in Colorado. Kaye is also surprised to find that a few tears are streaming down her cheeks. She struggles to collect herself and mumble a response about the cooking pot.

"Uh, yes, Michelle. I saw it on the top shelf in the hallway closet." Kaye takes the back of her hand while clearing her throat and quickly wipes the moisture from her cheeks. Kaye knows that her children still honor the memory of their father and she struggles daily to maintain that façade. However, there is evidence that Kaye still does not know the full extent of William's story.

Preparations for the evening meal came together very well. The dining room table is in a formal style. Anne designed and cooked a scrumptious menu, and the house is visitor-ready. Kaye, Michelle, Anne, and Dove-Whispering are nervous and fidgeting with last-minute clothes adjustments for each other. Their home is ready for their anticipated guests.

Ding-Dong...Ding-Dong...

"Hurry, Dove-Whispering, go to the door and see if it's Pamela and Dacia," Michelle says with both excitement and anxiety. Kiko, hearing the bell, immediately runs to the front door since she knows that the sounds trigger the arrival of a guest to the home. Dove-Whispering quickly follows her to the door since the two are inseparable. It is as though the pair exchange radar and sonar, whether in the swimming pool or walking through the house; each can detect what the other is thinking. Anne quickly reviews the menu. The kitchen temperature is hotter than a Nevada-based blacktop. The oven and the stove have been firing on high since early afternoon, and the dishes cooked to perfection, to Anne's liking. She has spared no culinary expertise on this introductory meal.

"Well, good afternoon, it's good to see you." Kiko and Dove-Whispering warmly greet the guests. Kiko instinctively knows that the visitors are welcomed and expected, barking her low-pitched welcome. Dacia and Dove-Whispering heartedly embrace as Pamela and Michelle welcome each other in a slightly more formal manner.

"Welcome to our home. We're glad that you accepted our invitation for dinner. Let's sit in the living room for a little while, it's a little more comfortable, and we can get to know each other," Michelle leads the small group into the front room for a casual conversation. Dacia and Pamela politely take their assigned seats in the accommodating environment. Kaye, Anne, and Michelle nervously position themselves around the guests so as to be attentive to their every word. Dove-Whispering exchanges a quick glance with Dacia which translates into, 'let's leave these ladies to talk about boring adult things.' Both girls jump up and quickly head for Dove-Whispering's bedroom at the back of the house, accompanied by Kiko. There they can talk about "all things girl" without the interruptions. They already know each other well enough to know that they are friends, Kiko quickly nudges against Dacia's leg to signal her acceptance into the pack. They don't need to 'get acquainted.'

"Dacia and I are glad that you're settling into BigTon so nicely. We have lived here all our lives; it's a very nice community. My parents owned a large apartment complex on the other side of town. When they died, I took over the ownership and had made it into a very nice business for myself and Dacia." Pamela could not believe that she felt so very comfortable with these new friends that she was spilling her life story out to them within minutes of entering their home. She is sure that they must think that she is a rather loose person who is free with her tongue and enjoys telling all that she knows. In reality, she is a quiet person and rather shy when meeting someone new. She doesn't know why she feels compelled to tell them about her family history. Maybe she feels nervous? Or, instinctively needs to hide something in her past? For some reason, she suddenly felt uncomfortable around her new friends.

"Well, Pamela, I am very glad that we moved to BigTon. Colorado is a beautiful state. Dove-Whispering and I are settling in okay, and she seems to be adjusting to school just fine. I know that the science class at school has helped her to adjust. We moved from Las Vegas, and the pace of life here is a little slower. We have time to take a breath now that we live here," Michelle says as she offers everyone some small drinks from a serving tray. "Besides, my job at the school district is going well. The district seems to ap-preciate the classroom teacher, and I feel like there is a po-tential for growth in my career here in the school district. Hopefully, we will be living in BigTon for many years."

Anne excuses herself from the living room to check on the meal. "The meal is ready, as mom used to say, 'the soups on,'" she peeks her head around the corner from the kitchen to let everyone know that the menu is ready.

"Let's go into the dining room," Kaye says. "Pamela, you and Dacia can sit here," as she motions to the opposite side of the table. Everyone else positions themselves in the empty chairs at the table. Each place setting arranged as it would have been when the Henry family was celebrating a particular holiday, Christmas, Easter, Mother's day.

"Gee, Grandma, this table looks just like it did for Christmas last year," Dove-Whispering blurted out as soon as she spies the festive setting.

"You are as observant as a wise ole' owl, sweetie. Yes, it is the same tablecloth, china, and silverware. We thought that it would make everyone feel at home, I'm glad that you like it." Kaye responds with a slight quiver in her voice. "I guess we all miss some of our happier days. It's good to have happy memories, but also we can go on and meet new friends like Pamela and Dacia who will help us make new memories. You'll see, sweetie. You and Dacia will discover that you have more in common than you realize. Before long you'll be best buddies." Kaye acknowledges what she wishes in her heart.

Pamela quickly chimes in, "I agree with your grandma, Dacia is looking forward to working with you on the science project this year. It's a tradition at the school. Each year the freshmen and incoming transfer students work together. It's a good project for all the incoming students to orient into the school environment. When I went to the school, there wasn't such a program, and the freshmen always seemed to have a hard time getting into the culture of the school. The school counselor, Ms. McKim-DePue and the science teacher, Ms. Walters developed the program."

"Oh yes, we met that goofy looking lady at school, that counselor lady. She has a weird name. I heard some of the kids in the locker room talk about her. They call her 'Stinky Poo.' She even looks like she has been at the school since they made the building. Every time I look around she is standing there looking at everybody. I'll bet that she knows everything that goes on at the school." Dove-Whispering found herself engaged in the conversation and talking quickly even though she and Dacia were still standing in the hallway.

"Well, she's been at the school ever since I attended. She indeed does seem to be everywhere. I noticed that she was watching me when I was a student. She knows everything that's going on at the school. No one knows her history, but she seems to be a permanent structure at the school. I think that she's involved with a couple of generations of students at this point. The school principal likes her. Yes, she does have a nickname, it's 'Stinky-Poo.' Everyone calls her that behind her back. It's not very nice." Pamela lowers her head, and the tone of her voice softens as she speaks. Almost as though she is ashamed, since she may have been part of the shaming of 'Stinky-Poo' during her high school days at Dakota Flats.

"Well, enough talk of the school. Let's all get seated at the table and enjoy the delicious meal. Let's enjoy Anne's special menu." Michelle states with authority as she guides the family and guests into the dining room.

Everyone gets situated at the dining room table. Kaye tentatively suggests that they say a short prayer before the meal. All agree by bowing their heads. Dove-Whispering and Dacia exchange snickers and smiles as they fold their hands and pretend to join in the stylized ritual. The adults politely mumble a few child-familiar monastic vows, and the group ends their recitations with a slight nod.

"Pamela, I hope that you don't think that I am too bold, but I would like to know a little more about your family. Since we are both single mother's and our daughters seem to be best friends, I would like to get to know you better." Michelle asks the question without making eye contact with Pamela since she feels a bit uneasy about the intrusion but is intent on learning all she can about her daughter's new friend.

"I am happy to share information about my family. The background about my parents is the real story. They came to Colorado when the silver rush was in full swing. Their vision was to develop some permanent housing for the residents. That's why they bought some land on the outskirts of BigTon and started a rooming house for the miners. That grew into a full-time boarding house for the residents. As the town grew, the Inn grew, both in size and reputation. Soon, the hotel was established and provided a good income for our family. My parents made sure that I learned the business as I grew up. When they passed away, I inherited the company. I now own the Inn and live there with Dacia." Pamela leans in toward the table and faces Michelle with an excited expression on her face in the thought that Michelle may also be ready to share aspects of her life.

"Wow, it sounds like you and your family are part of the "founding father's" of this town. You must know most of the business people and be aware of their backgrounds." Michelle says with a hint of nudging Pamela for more background information.

"Well, I guess that I know just about all the original people in this area. Recently though, the town is growing. Everyone has heard that it's a good place to live. The school district and Chamber of Commerce has grown in the past few years. I know a prominent leader of the chamber, Mr. Menendez; he is a family friend." Pamela is aware that she may be giving away too much personal information during this first meeting with her new friends. However, she does get a feeling that it's an environment in which it is safe to reveal a certain amount of her family history. There is still a tentative area around the fatherhood of Dacia, but she will not betray too much information in that area.

"It is good to meet someone who has such a strong connection to this community, Pamela. We feel so much more comfortable when we go back to Nevada knowing that Michelle and Dove-Whispering are friends with people who are so familiar with this area and its history." Kaye speaks with her usual tone of mother authority and grandmotherly concern.

"Oh mom, you always think that we are all still five years old," Anne replies in a half-kidding manner.

Finally, when Dove-Whispering can stand it no longer she speaks up, "I don't know about community things and history of people. I do know that we're hungry and I think that we should eat because Auntie Anne has made a delicious dessert and I can't wait to get a piece." Everyone agrees and picks up their napkins and silverware to begin devouring their meal.

Following the meal, Dacia and Dove-Whispering escape to the back bedroom with Kiko to play video games and talk about the new kids and things that they have met this year at high school, including Ms. McKim-DePue. The adults gravitate back into the dining room to enjoy their coffee and some conversation. Kaye decides that she wants to know just a little more about her daughter's new friend. Although there is no "red flag" identified from their relationship, Kaye senses that there is an underlying issue surrounding Pamela and her status in the community. So, Kaye takes a rather bold move at this point in the conversation.

"Pamela, both you and Michelle are single mothers. Do you mind me asking if Dacia's father is still in the picture for her? It may be none of my business. So, if you think that I'm too bold, just tell me so." Kaye is tentatively waiting for her answer and doesn't realize that she is holding her breath.

"I don't mind you asking me about Dacia's father. I do understand you being curious. I would be asking the same questions too. By the way, I do wonder about Dove-Whispering's father also, but didn't know when it would be polite to ask the question." Pamela realizes that she is talking fast and didn't intend to voice her question about Dove-Whispering's father.

"Her father doesn't live with us. He hasn't been in our lives for a few years. Dacia is very attached to him, and their personalities are very similar. She has his sense of humor, but her green eyes and fiery red hair must have come from a "long-lost-relative." I look a lot like my parents, but Dacia's features seem to come from her father's side of the family. I don't know much about his family of birth other than he grew up in the Midwest." Pamela guards against any further explanation of Dacia's father. She must tread lightly here. Today is her first meeting with this family, and even though they appear friendly, it is always good to err on the side of being conservative.

"Pamela, sometimes my mother can pry too much into others business. It's just because she is concerned about our safety. You should have seen her when we were kids. When we went out anywhere, we would have to answer a lot of questions: where we were going, who we would be with, how long we would be and what was the telephone number of where we would be so she could reach us. So, she finds that habit a little hard to break now that we are adults. I don't want you to feel like we are giving you the "third-degree" about your family or anything thing like that. It is none of our business unless you want to share." Michelle tries to reassure Pamela and "half-apologize" for her mother's prying attitude.

"I'm not embarrassed or concerned about your questions. It is only normal to wonder about Dacia's father. I also think about Dove-Whispering's father. Since our daughters will be spending a lot of time together, and they seem to have similar interests, we naturally want to know that they will be safe. It's not an issue for our daughters, but we, as parents, naturally would ask such questions. I have a good support network between my contact with the Chamber of Commerce members and my lifelong friends, so Dacia and I are never in need of friendships or support. However, you as new residents may feel a little lonely and want to make sure that things are safe and good. I understand." Pamela feels the tone of her voice reflect her defensiveness toward her daughter and is a little unsure as to the direction of this conversation.

"I apologize to you, Pamela. I tend to pry into others' business when it comes to my granddaughter. You are right, Michelle and Dove-Whispering are new to the area and need to form a support network. That can be an uneasy feeling. I hope that you and Dacia will be the base of the network for my daughter and granddaughter. I think that it will be a good, firm place to start." Kaye walks over to Pamela and bends down to offer her a friendly, social hug to represent a sign of understanding. The hug is accepted.

"Pamela, I am more than willing to share with you the background of Dove-Whispering's father. He is a man of questionable character who communicates with us only after some urging. He has missed most of Dove-Whispering's early years, and it left her with a mark of sadness. She carries many of his physical characteristics, her doe-brown eyes, and full-bodied, coffee-colored hair. She also has the tendency for silent observation when encountering a new or unknown situation, and this is a feature of her Native American background. Her height comes from my family, however, as does her interest in science and general knowledge. She is a happy, compassionate, intelligent teen with a keen interest in medicine and health." Michelle stops talking and realizes that she's proudly standing with her hands in the air, situated in the middle of her guests reciting a litany of her daughter's attributes as though she was singing the praises of a nationally known rock star or celebrated author. She doesn't apologize for her recitation.

"It seems as though the men in both of our families are fairly sparse. Dove-Whispering's grandpa, she called him " pa-pa," recently passed away and it left a big void in her life. In some ways, he filled the void left by her father. She spent a lot of time with him when she was younger and has good memories with him. It sounds like Dacia had a similar relationship with her dad in that she has good memories of her younger days with him." Michelle voices the obvious connection between the young girls, mentioning it almost as an afterthought.

"Yes, I guess they do. Almost like two peas in the same pod." Pamela nostalgically whispers as her thoughts momentarily drift back to the apartment that the three of them shared when Dacia was younger.

It's obvious that we all agree it's important to have father's and mother's in a young girl's life. However, the adults in these lives have done a good job in parenting these fine girls. Just as in nature when a young doe, or filly, or piglet or chick needs parenting or guidance the maternal instinct kicks into high gear and assumes both parenting duties. Often the small nestling grows to maturity but could still have benefited from the father influence." Kaye interjects into the discussion with the obvious statements since she feels that both Pamela and Michelle are feeling a little anxious about their past parenting situation.

"Pamela's father has not seen her for a couple of years. She doesn't know that he has passed away. Mr. Menendez, my close friend, informed me of the death, he was present at his death bed. I trust Mr. Menendez since he has been a family friend since my parents came to Colorado. I would implore you to hold that secret from Dacia until I can decide how to tell her of her dad's passing. She believes that he is just away on another one his extended trips, he took a lot of trips." Pamela's voice trails off into silence as she realizes she has just betrayed a family confidence to people that she doesn't know very well. She normally is not a risk taker, but this conversation about father's and daughters has brought down her natural defenses. She certainly didn't intend to reveal information about her family, especially something that she hasn't even shared with her daughter. Every bone in her body wants to take back her last statement; it betrays every principle that she holds sacred and true. However, it can't be taken back; it can't be untold. She will have to trust this new circle of friends to hold her confidence, at least until she has the strength to confront the issue with her daughter, Dacia. Her eyes tentatively meet the questioning gaze of both Michelle and Kaye, simultaneously. She notes a hint of understanding and sympathy. Could it be that these women understand such a delicate and personal issue?

"Oh, Pamela, I am so very sorry for your loss. I know what it is to have someone that you love pass away. My husband died a few years ago, and I still feel the loss. My children talk about happy memories of their time with him." Kaye responds quickly, sensing that the moment of silence following Pamela's disclosure is uncomfortable for everyone. Kaye is trying to prevent the dark veil of sadness from descending onto their previously happy conversation.

"He wasn't my husband, but he is Dacia's dad. Legal issues don't matter to Dacia; she just loves her father. She has memories of a person that she loves. Someday she will want to know details about her dad and how he passed away. Truthfully, I didn't want to know that information. When Mr. Menendez told me of her dad's passing, my whole world changed. I just wanted the pain to end." Pamela can hear herself giving out more information about her private life and can't believe that the details are still spilling out her mouth. She has already shared too much. Something unknown to her, allows the sharing of intimate life details to continue, restraining as she tries.

"Mr. Menendez has carried the burden of intense issues for our family. I'm not sure why he carries that load, but ever since he formed a relationship with my parents, he seems to have been a surrogate-protector in our lives. He gave me the news of Dacia's father passing away after he visited his hospital room in Nevada. I know that it was

an emotional time for Mr. Menendez. They formed a business relationship as well as a friendship." Pamela realizes
that she has already shared too much information about
her family with these newly met friends. She decides that
it's time to make a polite exit for her and Dacia. Pamela has
learned that in life it is not a good idea to reveal too much
information when one does not know all of "the players in
the game."

"Well, this is certainly a small world. My family has lived
in Nevada for many years. It is interesting that your friend,
Mr. Menendez has also visited that state and his business
partner also may have lived and worked in that area." Kaye
states with a note of nudging inquiry in her voice.

"It surely is a small world. The more people that I
meet, the more people I find have come from Nevada and
Arizona. I guess that those states sometimes get too hot for
some people. Colorado has a milder climate both in weather and politics. Our area here is certainly growing. I meet
new people all the time. Just like your family. Everyone is
looking for a fresh start." Pamela wants to end the conversation in a neutral tone without being nudged into revealing
more personal family information. She is beginning to feel
like there is a verbal bulldozer operating in this discussion.

"Don't worry about personal family information,
Pamela. My mother sometimes gets into areas where she
doesn't belong. You and I are just two mothers concerned
about our daughters. We'll be seeing a lot of each other
at school functions and possibly some social functions as
well. Revealing in-depth family histories isn't necessary
for us. Possibly, we'll become fast friends, and we can talk
about such things later, but that's just because we want to,

not because we're pressed into doing it." Michelle says with a sense of understanding. She stands next to Pamela with a compassionate hand on her shoulder. The two mothers exchange glances with a nod of understanding and the possibility of a future friendship.

"I think that it's time for Dacia and me to say good evening. It has been enjoyable to meet Dove's family and learn more about her background. It has been a full day for us and tomorrow is going to be just as busy." Pamela is cordial while trying to change the topic of death and fathers.

"It has been an enjoyable evening for all of us. The food was delicious, the company cordial and the conversation revealing. I'm sure that our relationship will continue to grow and our daughters will have a true friendship." Michelle's voice exudes a sense of understanding and sympathy.

Everyone adjusts their positions and walk toward Michelle's front door. Dacia and Dove-Whispering regrettably say their good-bye's next to Pamela's car in the driveway yet find it hard to separate from each other, pledging to meet again at school. Kaye and Anne say their farewell's to Pamela since they are leaving for Nevada the next day. Michelle and Pamela exchange multiple social hugs while vowing to contact each other concerning the next school function. The scene resembles a sheet of fly paper where the trapped insects vainly attempt to separate themselves from the adhesive yet continue to be drawn back into their desperate fate.

On the drive home to Nevada, Kaye and Anne briefly discuss their recent encounter with Pamela in Colorado. The main subject is Mr. Menendez's visit to Nevada when Dacia's dad is dying. "Mom, I wonder if the 'Mr. Menendez' that Pamela is talking about is related to the 'Mr. Menendez' that was Dad's boss. I know that the Menendez name is fairly common, and it's possible that the men aren't related. The way that Pamela talked, she knows the man very well, and he is a good family friend," Anne absent-mindedly rambles as though she doesn't expect an answer.

The atmosphere in the car fills with fantastic thoughts generated by two women frantically thinking of outrageous potential connections that obviously can't be made up of reality. Even the idea that "Pamela's, Mr. Menendez" and "William's, Mr. Menendez" can be the same "Mr. Menendez" is too preposterous even to consider. Neither woman will lend their voice to the idea.

Kaye and Anne spend the remainder of the drive back to Nevada with only superficial conversation. Each is trying to avoid the obvious, deeper topic. The implications of the two men being the same person are unthinkable. Anne wonders how could a person who knew her father in Nevada also know women in Colorado that she just met? They must be two different men with the same name. There are people in the world with the same last name that aren't related. That must be the answer. Sure. That's what it is. Her father was a trusted, honest man. He would never betray their family. He would never keep secrets from them – not her dad. What a foolish thought. She shakes her head as if to force the thoughts to fly out of her confused mind. It's as if she has a swarm of irritated bees aggravating all the little crevices of her brain. She suddenly wishes that they would have looked at the family photo album that her mom brought to Colorado while Dacia and Pamela were at the dinner.

CHAPTER 14
THE SCIENCE FAIR

"We need all hands on deck, and that means clearing hurdles for women and girls as they navigate careers in science, technology, engineering, and math."

Michelle Obama

"I didn't succumb to the stereotype that science wasn't for girls."

Sally Ride – Astronaut/Physicist

There are a few months left in the current school year. Ms. Walters is working with Dacia and Dove on their science project. The two girls chose to focus on a deoxyribonucleic acid (DNA) project. They consulted a variety of resources to decide on their project. Their main reference is a publication by Blaine T. Bettinger, "The Family Tree Guide to DNA Testing and Genetic Genealogy." Although this is a fairly detailed book, it is a basic resource to begin their project. Their first goal is to define the basic terms of their project. They want their project considered for state and regional competition, Dacia and Dove want to make sure that all guidelines are complete. To ensure that the judges will be able to understand all phases of their project, Dacia and Dove take special care to initially define the terms that they will use. Therefore, they describe the terms before they begin the project.

DNA is a component of a cell that controls the genetic functions for development and operation of each person. The nucleus, a control center of a cell, is the home for DNA. A small blueprint within the DNA called genes, create proteins, adenine, cytosine, guanine, and thymine. These proteins "pair-up" in specific ways. This specific pairing develops a **double-helix** form comprising into a chromosome. A chromosome pair contains one from each parent.

Each persons' genetic makeup is unique. This makeup, referred to as a karyotype, comprises twenty-two sets of chromosomes, a pair of sex chromosomes and rings of mitochondria (the powerhouse of the cell) mtDNA.

The yDNA passes from father to his son and determines the male gender.

The xDNA passes in a "double" process if the child is female, one from Mom, one from Dad. A male child will inherit one "X" chromosome, which comes from their mother.

The mtDNA passes from the mother to all children. However, only the female child can pass on this tendency.

The mtDNA tracing ends with the male child - it makes for a short family tree tracing.

If the mtDNA match and the yDNA match, then the two donors share a paternal ancestor.

The atDNA is twenty-two pairs of chromosomes, excluding non-sex chromosomes, that exist within the nucleus of each cell (autosomes). They are numbered based on their length and 22 of them, along with a marked sex chromosome, make up a haplogroup.

In testing the science project samples, the Short Tandem Report (STR) will be used, which is the sequences between (i.e.,.12 and 111 short segments) along with a chromosome. As well as the Single Nucleotide Polymorphism (SNP) which examines between (i.e. 1 and 100's) of single spots along the chromosomes.

This study will use the SNP process to look at the atDNA sequencing to determine genetic relatives. That means that hundreds of thousands of nucleotides, i.e., A-T-C-G will be tested along the DNA strand. A "MATCH" will determine a relative.

Dacia and Dove did their genetic homework and will be responsible for developing a "storyboard" and explaining and discussing these processes for the science fair competition.

Since Dacia and Dove are working together on the science project, they spend extensive time together at school. Their conversations involve school, the "weird" school counselor, boys, other girls, cool clothes and, of course, the science project. Neither has ever competed in a school-sponsored science competition, so both are nervous and feel unprepared. Ms. Walters, their science teacher, is allowed to clarify the rules and define the guidelines but the project must be developed and designed by the contestants. Of course, Ms. Walters wants her students to be successful and possibly win first place in the competition, but she also wants both girls to learn the basic rules of open, yet sometimes ruthless, competition.

"Well, girls, let's review the basic guidelines before we begin the project." Ms. Walters wants her two motivated science students to be aware of all aspects of their science project. She has guided other students through the science fair, and regrettably, some of them have placed last because they did not pay attention to all of the details. This time she wants both the project and the students to progress through the entire project, possibly even to win first place.

"I know, we need to read the directions before beginning." Both girls respond as if in unison. They seem to be already in-step with each other. Ms. Walters can't help but notice the difference yet the similarity of these two girls. One is graced with deep brown, coffee-colored hair and beckoning chocolate-shaded, almond eyes complimented with lightly tan skin. The other is endowed with a full head of fiery red, long curly hair, piercing green eyes and fragile, porcelain, almost translucent, skin. Even so, their personalities and abilities seem to compliment each other so very well. If their physical appearance wasn't so dramatic, she might think that they were meant to be twins.

"I know girls; you are starting to think with one brain. Even though you have already decided on your topic, you need to follow the rules. Therefore, we all need to be on the same page. I have read through the guidelines and am very familiar with the rules which are similar to previous years. What you both need to do is look at the outline carefully and memorize the rules so that you can repeat them in your sleep." Ms. Walters hands each girl a copy of the science fair outline. "Now keep this with you wherever you go." Ms. Walters tries to maintain her 'teacher tone' but is quickly thinking that these two students may turn out to be her most favorite science class members.

"Okay, we'll go over everything," Dacia and Dove answer again in unison. They take the science competition booklet and walk arm-in-arm into the crowded school hallway; they are like a pair of matched thoroughbreds pulling the winning chariot toward the finish line.

"We have to make sure that we know every twist and turn of this competition, Dacia." Dove states with faked authority.

"I know, Dove," Dacia chimes. "We want not only to win first prize for the school but to make a good showing in the regionals."

"Let's get together tonight and read everything," Dove suggests.

"Okay, We can meet at my house. My mother has a Chamber of Commerce meeting tonight, and we will have a couple of hours to look at everything," Dacia suggests.

"That's fine. I'll have my mom drop me off at your house when she gets off of work." Dove finalizes their plans with one last thought. "Dacia, can I bring my dog, Kiko over to your house with me. She gets a little lonely when I leave her for a long time. My mom will be busy grading school papers tonight. So, she'll be doing that stuff. Besides, Kiko has been with our family for a long time. When my "pa-pa" died a few years ago, she helped me feel better. I like to have her around."

"Sure you can, kiddo. We will have a good time. I like dogs," Dacia replies.

As the girls leave the school, the counselor meets them at the front door. "Well, girls. What is it that has you both so focused today?" Dacia and Dove hadn't noticed Ms. McKim-DePue until she steps directly in front of them. The counselor seems to have a knack for showing up when least expected. It's as though she lurks in the shadows of the school and pops out every time someone is in the middle of a private or secret conversation, like the 'coo-coo' of an old fashioned clock.

Of course, neither girl has any intention of telling 'Stinky Poo' the true meaning of their conversation. "Well, uh, we, uh, were, uh, just talking about science class. Yes, that's what it was, science class. Our teacher wants us to be good students in the class." Dacia offers a weak answer without making eye contact with the intimidating counselor while Dove fumbles with the outline of the science project.

"Well, you know girls that I am interested in all the students. Especially students that are working on the science projects. I have been watching you, two girls. You are working together, easily. The school has been competing in that contest for years. You know, Dacia, when your mother went to this school, she also worked on the project. She liked science and was a good student." The counselor adjusts her position so that she is now standing directly in front of

Dacia and attempting to adjust her facial position so that their eye contact is unavoidable.

"You have been at the school a long time haven't you, Ms. McKim-DePue?" Dacia says while trying, without success, to avoid looking the counselor straight into her eyes.

"Yes, I have, Miss Dacia, many years. I watched your mother grow up here." Ms. McKim-Depue says with a confused mixture of pride, sorrow, and authority.

"Wow, that is a long time." Dacia and Dove, again answer in unison.

"Yes, a very long time. But it has passed quickly. I keep busy." Ms. McKim-DePue answers as if her memories and speech seem to become entangled.

"We need to get home now. Ms. Walters wants us to review the science competition guidelines. Bye now." Dacia and Dove again answer in unison and walk quickly past the counselor, hitting the "panic bar" of the front door without waiting for a reply. They felt like two convicts escaping from a maximum security prison.

"Wow, that was a close call," Dove giggles with breathless irritation.

"Yeah, I thought for a minute that 'Stinky-Poo' was going to put her hands on me and confess some long-held secret. That was creepy," Dacia concedes while considering that some truth may hide in the counselor's behavior, she keeps that thought to herself.

━┽ ┾━

As Dove-Whispering rides in Michelle's car with Kiko to Dacia's house, she remembers her drive from Nevada to

Colorado. During that ride with her Uncle Benedict, emotions overwhelm her when talking about her "pa-pa." Her uncle understood that emotions often could become too big for her. Dove-Whispering and her uncle talked about such things – the things of emotions and feelings. Normally, she would keep those thoughts inside so that she wouldn't get all tangled up in them. That's just how she was; it's how she had always been. Maybe it was the Native American part of her that seemed to bring out the emotional side. Whatever it was, she found it hard to talk about her feelings, except with her Uncle Benedict. Just for a moment, she wants to talk to her uncle; but just having her loving Kiko by her side eases her discomfort. The feeling fades, like the sting of the morning sun burning the pre-dawn fog over a bayou.

Her mom pulls the car up to Dacia's, which is an apartment complex and everyone walks up to the front door. Kiko lets out a low, moaning howl as if to signal a welcoming, hello. Michelle rings the doorbell which strikes a friendly chime. Dacia cheerfully opens the door followed closely behind by Pamela.

"Welcome everyone, come in. Dove, Dacia has been waiting for you. She put the paperwork on the kitchen table. I was going to my Chamber of Commerce meeting this evening but canceled that because I wanted to greet both of you this evening." Pamela greets them with a welcoming smile and a courteous manner as she invites them to sit for a while.

"I am behind in my school work. There are a lot of papers to grade. I can't stay long, just for a little chat." Michelle answers in an apologetic tone. "But I am curious about the apartment complex here. Do you own the whole area? It certainly is a lot to manage."

"Yes. My family built it in the 1900's when the silver and gold discoveries were booming in this area. They expanded on the initial building until it grew to its present size. I worked here ever since I was a young child. My parents wanted me to learn all parts of the business. When they died, I inherited the company. I have only a few full-time helpers, and my associates from the Chamber of Commerce do a lot of tasks for me. Other than that, I manage very well. Some day Dacia will be able to work here as well." Pamela answers with obvious pride.

"You should be very proud of your family's accomplishment. It is a firm business, a heritage that can be passed down to future generations. Do you have a lot of residents? Are your rooms usually full?" Michelle asks with a note of inquiry that makes her feel as though she is too much like her mother, Kaye.

"We enjoy total occupancy on a regular basis. In fact, Dacia's father came here a few years ago. He was only going to stay for a couple of weeks, but things changed, and he obviously ended up staying much longer. It was a good arrangement for everyone. But enough talking about me. What about your family? Did they make it back to Nevada okay?" Pamela quickly tries to change the topic of discussion since the topic of William stirs some unpleasant memories.

"Yes, my mother and sister returned to Nevada just fine. They enjoyed their stay in Colorado. Their visit to the high school was helpful in understanding Dove's relationship within the community. Both my mom and sister feel confident toward the relocation of our family into this area.

They will be back for another visit. Although they feel that part of our family has migrated to another land, much like an early explorer that paves an uncharted path through the wilderness to find a new, undiscovered land." However, Michelle reassures Pamela that first impressions have been positive.

Just as Pamela's and Michelle's conversation is fading into a generic focus, there is a loud, growling, snarling sound coming from the back part of the house. Two startled mothers respond to the source of the disturbance, Dove and Dacia are already at the scene. Kiko postures herself in an attack position in front of a bedroom closet snarling and growling at an unseen creature inside the enclosure. Possibly a snake or scorpion has escaped into the corner of the closet and Kiko is determined to route it out, a protector of the hearth.

"Kiko, what are you doing? What is in the closet? Kiko, sit." Dove sends a firm, verbal command to her trusted companion. The obedient dog hesitates, quickly shoots a confused look up to her master and resumes her protective stance.

"Your dog seems confused, Dove," Dacia says with an obvious quiver in her voice. "There is nothing in that closet. We just store old family stuff in there." Dacia's voice trails off as she backs away from the scene not trusting the canine's temperament.

Dove slowly approaches Kiko and takes a firm grip on her neck collar. Kiko instantly relaxes her stance yet maintains her vigilance, as though she's sitting at a traffic light waiting for the green light to shine.

Pamela slowly approaches the closet door and after eyeing the attentive dog opens the sliding door as though she half-expects a wind-up toy to jump out from the dark enclosure.

The interior reveals a collection of discarded men's clothing, shirts, pants, shoes, socks, gloves and hats, all well used. There is nothing obviously threatening in the closet. However, Kiko maintains her guard while sniffing and looking as though she is searching for the familiar object. The dog seems confused as though she has "cornered the fox but can't locate it."

"Pamela, what do you keep in this closet?" Michelle quickly shouts. "Kiko is telling us that she recognizes something in here."

"Nothing of value. It's some of my husband's old clothes. I can't seem to get rid of them. Of course, he won't need them, but sometimes I just come here and run my fingers over the clothes and smell his scent in the shirts. It reminds me of him." Pamela runs her fingers over the shirts hanging in the closet as he buries her body in the clothing. It is embarrassing how quickly she becomes enveloped within the apparel, unaware of the others remaining in the room, as though the clothing transforms Pamela back into another reality.

"Pamela," Michelle shouts out her name, as though to break the spell.

"Uh, Oh, I'm sorry. I didn't mean to do that. My husband isn't here. Michelle, we need to talk about something," Pamela leaves the room and motions for Michelle to follow her to the kitchen. Dacia, Dove, and Kiko remain standing in front of the closet attempting to unravel the scene like hungry baby chicks waiting for meal time.

Pamela and Michelle sit at the kitchen table for a quick discussion about the disappearance of Dacia's father, "Dacia doesn't know that her father died. She thinks that he is on another one of his out-of-town trips. Although, he's been gone a long time, a couple of years. I'm sure that she is getting curious. She'll start asking questions any day now. That's all I want to say now, but we can talk later." Pamela offers a potential long-term friendship with Michelle.

"I understand, Pamela. I lost my father a couple of years ago, also. It is hard to get rid of personal items that belong to him. His shirts in your closet look very similar to my dad's shirts, so I guess that their personalities were similar. That means that they were the type of man who could develop a close relationship with others. The type of person who could make you believe that you were "his one-and-only." I understand why it is difficult to let go of his memory. It is hard for me also. I certainly will keep your secret about Dacia's dad. We can talk about it later and other things whenever you need." Michelle touches Pamela's shoulder as she makes eye contact to relay a sense of compassion and understanding.

Michelle checks on Dove and Kiko and see's that they are enjoying relaxing music in Dacia's bedroom. She understands that Pamela is a new friend and her daughter, Dove has begun a new chapter in her life. Michelle overhears their conversation, "I was surprised to see Kiko react like that, Dacia. She does get excited when she senses family things". Kiko is attached to us. Why my dog reacted to the clothes in your closet is a real mystery to me," Dove's statement is more like a litany of past events rather than an apology for Kiko's behavior. The aftermath of the incident floats in the air like a low-lying cloud signaling the coming of a thunderstorm with no hint of a spring-time breeze to blow the cloud away.

⇒⊹ ⊹⇐

Dacia and Dove have reviewed the science project guidelines. Ms. Walters arranges with Mr. Menendez of the Chamber of Commerce, to have a local laboratory provide the needed supplies for the project. The list contains a variety of both medical and testing equipment. After an in-depth discussion with Ms. Walters and the laboratory, both girls decide that each will supply the first two samples of DNA to begin the project.

The goal of the project is to take random saliva samples of ten additional fellow students. The samples are grouped in sets of two. The names of each student are assigned a "number." Therefore, no one knows which DNA sample connects to which student. The samples are traceable only by an identification number. The goal of the project is to match the donor pair's DNA. Dove and Dacia want to determine if any of the matched sets are related, they don't expect matches. Since the participants are students, Dacia, Dove, and Ms. Walters compile a parental permission form. This form outlines the project guidelines and result potential. The surprise is that all the permission forms are received back with signed parental signatures.

⇒⊹ ⊹⇐

Ms. McKim-DePue, the school counselor, and Mr. Menendez, from the Chamber of Commerce, who has worked on the high school science project from years past, decide to meet each other under the pretense of securing additional supplies for the project. However, the true reason for their meeting is more sinister and suspicious than science supplies. They meet off school grounds so as not to arouse the typical gossipy tongues of a small community.

"I guess that you know what this means. We may finally be exposed. The whole issue will be revealed. The lies and secrets will be known in one instant. What are we to do? I don't think that I can handle it after all these years. Everyone will know what happened so many years ago." Ms. McKim-DePue is shaking as she speaks frankly with her long time friend and confidant, Mr. Menendez. They sit under the shade tree that has concealed so many of their secluded and clandestine conversations over the torturous years. This time it's different. The truth is closer, more damaging; as though it were a hungry bear searching for a beehive dripping with fresh, sweet honey.

"Don't worry. We have worked with issues like this before. The truth is only for us. We can keep it that way. No one will know about Pamela. Trust me. I have always guided you. We will work together on this matter, too. No one knows about William, and no one will find out about Pamela, either. We are both good at keeping secrets. This little science project isn't going to change anything. Now calm yourself. We have come so far. We can do this. Life is good, and people are doing fine. Don't worry." Mr. Menendez places a reassuring hand on 'Stinky Poo's shoulder and feels her calm composure return. The school counselor doesn't often reveal her emotional side, not concerning personal matters. However, Mr. Menendez has been her confident since her teenage years and guided her through life in a positive way. She is not about to sway away from his advice at this point in her life.

'Stinky-Poo' and Mr. Menendez resume their respective positions within the community with no hint of their meeting. Whatever their secretive issues are, they won't be known this day.

Mr. Menendez reflects on the decisions he has made over the past few years. It's time for him to look through the lens of his life. His thoughts turn toward William's family in Nevada. Following William's death, there remain unanswered questions that he knows will devastate lives, and he holds the answers. The people who are in his professional and personal life could also be in for some heartfelt news. This lens through which he is looking doesn't give him a clear vision. Instead, it reveals a kaleidoscope tangled with emotions and questions that have been weaving themselves into a snare for the past few years. He doesn't like the picture, doesn't like it at all.

⇒ ⇐

Dacia and Dove take the saliva samples for the science project. Ms. Walters supervises the collection of the other donors. All of the samples are assigned a generic number, and the process is explained again to the donors. The actual processing of the samples occurs at a State Certified Lab that coordinates with the school district. Although the matching process is explained and displayed by Dacia and

Dove on their storyboards for the science competition, the girls will also present the numbered lab results for judging. Both girls are responsible for understanding and explaining the processing of the DNA results if questioned by the judges. Normally, the DNA results will be available in a few days. However, this is a busy state lab, and the school samples are only a part of their workload. Therefore, the results will be available in two to three weeks, just in time to meet the science competition guidelines.

CHAPTER 15
FINALLY THE TRUTH

*"Truth is like the sun. You can shut it out
for a time, but it ain't going away."*

Elvis Presley

*"Above all, don't lie to yourself. The man
who lies to himself and listens to his lies comes
to the point that he cannot distinguish the
truth within him and around him, and so
loses all respect for himself and others. And
having no respect, he ceases to love."*

**Fyodor Dostoyevsky,
The Brothers Karamazov**

Ms. Walters is coordinating the information between the state-run laboratory and the science class at Dakota Flats High School. She is making sure that all information for the upcoming science fair at the school is timely and accurate. What she does not know is that Mr. Menendez is also working with the laboratory to delay the progress of the program. He is talking with the supervisor of the laboratory services to double-check all results. His purpose is to not only delay the program but also make sure that the findings are correct. Mr. Menendez has an alternative motive. He promised his longtime friend and confidant, Ms. McKim-DePue to keep their secret, and that it must be kept was decided so many years ago. A secret that would shake the very structure, of not only Dakota Flats High School, but also the community of BigTon to its very core. It was not a conspiracy; it did not involve a crime against anyone. Responsible parties agreed that it was better to withhold damaging information from people who did not need to know.

However, so many things had changed in this once small town. BigTon was now a bustling community. New families with new ideas moved into the area. Somehow, the old ideas of privacy, truth, and honesty seem to have changed with the new influx of people. What once was true did not seem to matter in these new times.

Oh, how he struggles with his conscious. It is as though he is a piece of untreated wood and a ravenous swarm of termites is feasting on him as their last meal on earth. He feels as though the years are creeping up on him, unnoticed. He holds such a large storehouse of information in his brain. He knows too much. He has done too much.

What will he do if these two naïve, innocent, pupils reveal the past? Their eager attempts to delve into the depth of their beloved science would change their lives in ways that they could not imagine. Mr. Menendez cared for all the people involved in the situation, but he knew that they would be surprised, shocked, and hurt. He could not discuss his concerns with anyone because the two men who caused the incidents so many years ago were now dead, and they died unrepentantly.

He witnessed the pain on Pamela's face when he told her of the situation surrounding William's death. It was as though he had driven a dagger into her heart. Pamela's look of betrayal toward him imprinted on the retina of his brain. Simply closing his eyes recalled her facial expression of hurt, pain, and disbelief. William's betrayal was everlasting. It would not take Pamela long to ask more questions, questions about William. She would want to know what he knew about William and how long he knew it. Oh, Mr. Menendez knew that he might be hard pressed to face that interrogation.

However, there was an even greater inquisition facing the aging community leader, and he dreaded it, even more, the secret that the science project would surely reveal. The school counselor and the Chamber of Commerce captain made that pact of silence long ago. Many secret rendezvous have passed to keep that transaction hidden from the public eye. History and time held the past in an iron-clad box. The contents would not be understood; especially if they were pried open and splattered onto unsuspecting lives. It would be as if the erupting volcano spewed hot molten lava onto a village town and destroyed the humble inhabitants. Mr. Menendez knew that he would have to answer for that revelation, it was his decision so many years ago. The proverbial clock was ticking, and he couldn't hold back the time, just like progress, it just keeps moving forward.

⇥ ⇤

"Well, Mr. Menendez, how are you doing today?" Ms. Walters greets him warmly as they meet in the teacher's lounge at the high school. "I'm glad that we could meet here today to review some final details of the science projects. It seems like the actual testing of the samples hasn't begun at the lab yet. The laboratory manager said that you wanted to go over some final items with him first."

"Uh, yes, uh, I just want to be sure of all the legal issues. I know that we did get the permission slips from the parents, but sometimes it's the small details that get overlooked." Mr. Menendez averts Ms. Walters eye contact knowing that she may detect that he is not being honest in his reason for wanting to delay the process.

"I do understand that, but we need to move along quickly, or we will miss the science fair deadline. There is a timeline of two weeks for the return of the results, and we are right at the margin today. Could you talk with the laboratory manager later today and finalize any legal issues?" Ms. Walters' voice harbors a hint of urgency with sprinkles of suspicion as though she is seasoning a stew and isn't quite sure how much cayenne pepper is needed.

"Yes, I will do that today." Mr. Menendez answers quickly so as not to arouse the science teacher's suspicion. His brain is racing to pinpoint new options to use as delay tactics, as he is quickly running out of reasonable choices.

"Do you see anything else that we missed. We have monitored this science fair for many years; we should know the details in our sleep by now, like sleep walking. The guidelines are the same as in previous years." Ms. Walters states with a finality in her voice as though it's time to adjourn and there shouldn't be any further delays.

"I didn't know that you were going to be here today," said Ms. McKim-DePue as she taps Mr. Menendez on the shoulder as he reaches the front door of Dakota Flats High School. He turns as though someone has caught him committing a crime. The school counselor jumps in response to his reaction but their face-to-face encounter, although quick, tells a revealing story. Eye contact is quickly averted and both the school counselor and the community leader part company. Ms. McKim-DePue visually searches the school hallway to detect if any of the school staff or students witnessed the exchange, she does not detect a witness.

"Whoa, did you see that?" Dacia whispers to Dove as they exit science class.

"No, what?" Dove says absent-mindedly.

"Really, kid?" Dacia says in disbelief.

"No, what?" Dove says with exasperation.

"The two at the front door. It is as if someone caught 'em smoking a joint or something. Wow. 'Stinky-Poo' and Mr. Menendez. Talking but not talking. It was weird. They bumped into each other but pretend that they didn't see each other," Dacia says with an air of confusion.

"Well, maybe they don't want the students to know that they know each other. Grownups are funny about things like that. My mom does stuff like that sometimes when she doesn't want me to know things." Dove says with a slight tinge of knowledge to her speech.

"I know, sometimes when my mom and Mr. Menendez talk about things, and they don't want me to hear, they pretend that they are talking about something else when I come into the room, but I always know what's up." Dacia doesn't expect an answer.

"Well, when this science project is over, Mr. Menendez won't be hanging around school anymore, and life can go back to normal. You and I can do friend's stuff and not be so involved in this science fair competition. Our moms like each other and we will be friends for a long time. Nothing will change that." Dove states with a sense of confidence.

"That's it, Dove, friends forever. Nothing will change."

"Hi, grandma. I am doing fine. No, the results are not back yet from the lab for our science project. We should be getting them in the next two days. I am excited to see if all of our research is correct and if we find the results, we want. We do not expect that any of the "paired" students will be related. Our storyboard is ready, and Dacia and I know the research so we can explain it to the judges." Dove-Whispering's phone conversation with Kaye ends as Anne interrupts to talk with Dove-Whispering about shopping and recipes.

"So, Dove-Whispering, are you and your friend Dacia getting along? Do you like the same kind of clothes? Do you both really like science? I found a new recipe for cookies that we should try when I see you again." Anne is so excited to talk with Dove-Whispering that she does not give the teen time to answer the questions she keeps shooting at her.

"Auntie wait. You talk too fast. I have to tell you about a thing that happened at school. It is about this person Mr. Menendez and that weird school counselor, 'Stinky-Poo.' You remember her from the parent-teacher night?"

"Yes, she was very interested in talking with Dacia and Ms. Love. That counselor also was hanging around and talking a lot to the science teacher." Kaye states to nudge Dove-Whispering into telling more of the story.

"Those two people met each other by the front door of the school but pretended that they didn't know each other. Both of them were nervous and anxious as if they were hiding something important. Dacia and I were the only ones who saw them, and it was spooky. I do not understand why they could not just say hello to each other and then go on about what they were doing. Oh, well. It's just weird." Dove still sounds confused.

"I know kid. Grown-ups are just weird sometimes. Well, I can't wait to hear the results of your science project. Call us as soon as you know." Anne's excited tone pleases Dove-Whispering

"I will auntie. Love ya. Bye." Dove-Whispering smiles as she hangs up the phone.

—◁+ +▷—

The results of the DNA testing are complete. However, the manager at the laboratory wants the science teacher to know that even though each sample is tagged generic, there is a "matched pair." A matched pair indicates that two DNA samples are from students who are genetically related. The community of BigTon is a small, growing area and the high school within the town is a microcosm of the town, and everyone knows everyone. No one expected any of the students to be related.

Before any of the science project results can be released, the science teacher, Ms. Walters convenes a meeting with the state laboratory manager, Mr. Menendez, the school principal, the school counselor and herself. All of the parents and the involved students signed a release form before participating in the science project. This form released the school, the staff, and its personnel from any liability associated with the test. Therefore, no one is concerned about legal issues. However, they want to discuss the unexpected "matched" pair.

"Well, this is surely a surprise. Since all of the samples have numbers, there is no way to tell which pair of students is the "matched" pair." Ms. Walters states when all of the concerned members convene.

"That's not necessarily true," the laboratory manager responds. "The first two numbered samples are the "standards," and they are known. Sample #1 is Dacia Love, and Sample #2 is Dove-Whispering Henry. I also have further information. Those are the two "paired" samples."

"Oh, my. Are you telling us that Dacia and Dove-Whispering are related? That's not possible. They don't even look alike. They come from different parts of the country. Their mothers didn't know each other before moving here. I have known Pamela Love since she was a child and I would have known." Ms. Walters states in disbelief, lets out a heavy sigh and sits back in her chair.

Ms. Walters stands up again. She is trying to put into words the mixture of feelings raging inside of her. "I'm at a loss for words. This kind of thing can't be happening at Dakota Flats. I know that DNA tells the truth, but this time something is out of place." Ms. Walters sits down again still shaking her head. Her normal professional composure is gone and quickly being replaced with the stooped stature of a confused female.

"Uh, well, we need to think about the student's parents. Who will notify them? I don't know if they understand the tests, but they need to know what the results indicate. It may well cause them some concern, but it needs doing." The laboratory manager is direct with his statement. He stands at the head of the conference table looking squarely at each of the members searching for an answer.

"Why, yes, we must notify the parents. It is our duty." The principal answers as though he is a parrot reciting a practiced sermon.

Ms. McKim-DePue and Mr. Menendez remain quiet yet adjust their positions often. It is obvious to the assemblage by their uncomfortable actions that the normally talkative leaders may know something more about the situation.

Mr. Menendez clears his throat so as to attract attention, pushes his chair deliberately back from the table and slowly stands. "I believe that we need to contact the two sets of mothers and students involved in this science project before we go any further with this discussion. There is obviously some sensitive information involved here. I also hope that

I do not need to mention that we are all professionals and sworn to bonds of secrecy about these kinds of issues. Since Ms. McKim-Depue and I are judges for the science fair, we need to make some hard and significant decisions about the submission of our entry into the competition. I suggest that since Ms. Walters is working with the science fair, she knows the students and is well acquainted with both of the mothers; she should be the one who contacts them to come in for a meeting to discuss the science fair. She could tell them it is to talk about some of the initial test results. We can all attend the meeting, or she can meet with them alone, whatever we decide." Mr. Menendez stands quietly for a second in front of his longtime friends as if in a trance, folds his hands across his chest, lowers his head and slowly regains his seat.

At this point, Ms. Walters clears her throat, although, with some difficulty, standing seems to be beyond her capacity. "Since I seem to be the most logical person to contact the mothers and students in this situation, I will. Unless there is further discussion needed on the subject." She quickly makes eye contact with each member of the group, all avert eye contact and mumble incoherent sentences with various degrees of head movement.

The meeting adjourns with a sense of relief for all members except Ms. Walters. She has the burden of contacting Ms. Love and Ms. Henry concerning the initial results of the science fair. It is not a job she relishes. She contacts them immediately to resolve the issue.

"Well, I can't imagine why I'm here. You already have my signature on the permission form for the science fair. Ms. Walters was rather vague when she called me. It seems that there are a few issues that have occurred that we need to discuss. It all seems rather hush, hush, if you ask me." Ms. Henry nervously adjusts her position in the chair as she faces the same members who met in the same room a few days earlier discussing the same issue, unknowingly, she is now part of that decision-making group.

All eyes immediately focus on the slowly opening door as it reveals the partial view of a professionally dressed, Ms. Love. "Am I in the right room? The lady at the front desk directed me to this conference room. I'm here for the meeting about the science fair." Pamela continues her entrance into the room and quietly selects a seat close to the door. The scene resembles a carton of newly hatched, fragile eggs teetering on the edge of a kitchen table.

"Why yes. We ask both of you ladies here today to discuss some of the initial results of the science fair." Let us introduce ourselves, each member of the assemblage takes their turn to introduce themselves to the mothers. Then the group's unofficial spokesperson, Mr. Menendez reluctantly rises to his feet to present the heart of the issue. "Let me begin by saying that anything that we discuss here is confidential. I also want to say that if anyone has something to add to the discussion that we respect each other and take turns to discuss issues. With that said, I want to get to the heart of the matter. The first two DNA paired samples for the science fair are intentionally marked with the donor's name so that we can secretly trace the accuracy of the test. So, those samples not only have numbers but names assigned to them. Therefore, we know information about those first two donors, we know that they are genetically related."

The room is silent as though a glass light bulb has fallen from its socket and everyone is waiting to hear the noise of crystal shards crashing to the grounds, the expectation is touchable. The silence breaks like a dry, brittle stick when both mothers respond in unison, much like their daughters had done. "What, what are you saying? Did you call us here to say that our daughters are related? That's impossible." Pamela and Michelle shoot a net of suspicion toward each other, oblivious to others' presence.

"Before we go any further, let's take a moment to consider our next step," Mr. Menendez interrupts. "I need to remind everyone again that whatever we say at this meeting is held to the strict privacy standard that we discussed. Ms. Henry and Ms. Love that means we will not talk about any part of this meeting to anyone outside of this room."

"Wait just a minute. You just called that woman Ms. Henry! You just called Dove's mother, Ms. Henry. I didn't know Michelle's last name until this very minute. It can't be true. Dacia's dad's last name is 'Henry.' We all need just to stop talking a minute." Pamela stands up, walks indignantly around the conference table, repeatedly stamping her feet and mumbling incoherently.

Michelle places her hands flatly and firmly on the table, ignoring Pamela's reactions, violently pushing her chair back from the table. "I will not stay here and listen to my family being talked about in front of everyone. If there is something that needs discussion, then I am willing to meet with the manager of the state laboratory and Mr. Menendez. I also need to talk with my family about this issue. I see no further need to continue with this meeting. You may contact me at my home." Michelle leaves the conference room followed closely by Mr. Menendez. Two mothers with a previous friendship, part company perchance to meet later for discussion concerning their shared lineage.

⇒⊹ ⊹⇐

Mr. Menendez and the school counselor quickly approach Michelle before the upset woman reaches the front door of the high school. "Uh, Ms. Henry, could you wait just a minute? We would like to talk with you." Michelle stops in her tracks, swivels on her feet and flashes them a look filled with hurt, disbelief, anger, and pain. It was as if she was standing in the path of exploding, molten lava, and there was no escape, and she was going to be burned alive.

"There are some issues to talk about concerning your family and the science fair. None of us expected these results from the DNA testing. I can't imagine that you believed there would be any positive matches when you signed the parental consent form." Mr. Menendez tries to maintain eye contact with the distressed mother as she shifts her weight from one foot to another as she sways from left to right, attempting to avoid the inevitable conversation.

"Ms. Henry, I watch both girls every day in school and see that they have a strong friendship. I know that whatever comes out of this situation will be okay, as long as everyone can just talk about the issues." Ms. McKim-DePue attempts to calm the mother of students that the school counselor has come to know well. 'Stinky Poo' was confident that this intense issue could be seen as a good situation instead of something threatening and intense if only the mothers and daughters could sit and talk.

"Right now, I can't talk about this. I don't know what Ms. Love wants to do, but this is something I can't handle right now. It's terrible. People better not find out about this. Everybody better keep it a secret. It's none of their business." Michelle slams her hand on the panic bar on the front door of the school and pushes out of the entrance, running to her car.

Mr. Menendez and Ms. McKim-Depue disheartened, return to the conference room where the school principal and Ms. Walters are involved in a loud discussion with Ms. Love. "Well, maybe something went wrong with the testing process. Mistakes are made every day with everything. Call the lab and ask about the tests."

"Ms. Love, the results are always double checked before they report them. Therefore, we know that they are correct. We need to address the issue." Ms. Walters sits next to a mother who is learning that her family's genetics has changed by a factor unknown to her. A family secret is now known that Pamela didn't know was hidden. Her shame is that the revelation is public. Pamela has not yet talked with Dacia about the death of her father, and now she's confronted with an even greater issue, the very genetics of their family.

Both Pamela and Michelle decide to talk with their daughters when they come home from school. The members in the conference room, who are present when Pamela and Michelle are given the results of the DNA tests, vow to keep the information secret. All agree that the information is a private family matter and doesn't need discussion within the public perv.

"Mom, I was called to school today by the principal. I met with a group of people to discuss the DNA results of

Dove-Whispering's science fair project. Remember when I was asked to sign the parental consent form? Well, that's why I met with the group today. The results show that Dove-Whispering's companion is Dacia. She and Dove-Whispering are related." Michelle waits silently for her mother's reaction.

"What! What the hell are you saying? Somebody is playing a trick on you, Michelle. That can't be true. Those two girls have never met each other before now. How could something like that be true? Our two families don't even live in the same town. What are you going to do about all of this, Michelle?" Kaye is still breathing heavily after her verbal explosion.

"Mom, I remember one thing that Ms. Love said. I guess that she was surprised that our last name is 'Henry.' Pamela seems focused on that fact. I imagined that it meant something to her. I know that her last name is 'Love.' Does that mean anything to you?" Again Michelle waits to see if there is a clue in her mother's answer.

"Michelle, did you say 'Love'? Did you say that Pamela's last name is 'Love'? It can't be. It's not possible. Such a thing would not happen." Kaye fell silent on the other end of the phone line.

"Mom. Mom, are you there? Mom, what's going on?" Michelle is listening to a crackling sound on the phone line.

"Michelle, do you remember when I found your father's papers from his employment in Colorado? It was after his funeral, and I found his briefcase in his office. Well, the name of his letters to his girlfriend was Pamela Love. He was living with her in Colorado. I wonder if this Pamela is the same, Pamela? It can't be!" Now Kaye is listening to a silent telephone line, and, she waits.

"Let me get your sister, Anne on the phone; she needs to hear this too. I want us all to hear this together. If it turns out that this woman is the 'Pamela,' then we all need to hear about it. I wish that we could get Benedict on this phone party also, but not now. Anne, come here."

"What is it, mom?" Anne asks.

"Michelle has something that we all need to hear. It is about Dad's old girlfriend. Remember that girl Pamela Love? Well, it seems that she is the mother of Dove-Whispering's new school friend. Michelle is on the phone telling us about it." Kaye picks up the phone in the kitchen so that all three Henry women can hear the news first-hand.

"OKAY, say it again, Michelle. This scandalous information about the 'Love' woman is something that we all need to know." Kaye says with an unusual sense of bitterness.

"I was called to school today to get the results of the DNA tests for the science fair. The first two "paired" students were Dacia and Dove-Whispering. Well, the results showed that pair was "positive", meaning that the two students are related. All the leaders of the school and some of the main science fair judges were at this meeting. So they all know the information. Everyone is a professional and bound to a bond of secrecy so they can't talk about it to anyone. Pamela Love was also at the meeting. I imagine that this was all new information to her also. I left as soon as I got the results but I know that we all need to talk about it." Michelle exhales a deep breath of near exhaustion after the detailed speech.

"Do the girls know?" Kaye asks.

"What girls?" Michelle quickly retorts.

"Dacia and Dove-Whispering, of course," Kaye responds.

"Not yet, but I didn't think of them until just now," Michelle says.

"Don't worry about them. We'll talk to both of the girls about all of this as soon as we find out the whole story. I have a lot of anger toward this incident and your father that I still need to get through. First, we need to deal with this issue of the matching DNA results. Michelle, I want you to set up a meeting with Pamela and talk to her as a mother. That way she won't be suspicious or concerned. She'll believe that you are thinking about the girls." Kaye is trying to nudge her daughter into getting the issues resolved quickly.

"Okay, Mom, I'll call Ms. Love tonight. I'm not sure what to tell Dove-Whispering." Michelle says good-bye to her mom and sister and hangs up the phone feeling overwhelmed and uncertain. It's as though a poisonous snake has just wound itself around the tree limb that supports her firmly built nest and it's ready to consume not only the adult birds but all the precious little chicks within.

Mr. Menendez has never faced a situation like this one. His life is coming full circle. As he sits with his wife of many years at the kitchen table, the mood is somber yet relaxed. There is a sense of finality about the day.

"Honey, is there bothering you? Sometimes you bother me. I think that you carry a heavy load. Your job is complicated, and you are responsible for managing many people. I know that the death of William still bothers you. You were close to him, like a very close friend. I worry about you, dear." Mrs. Menendez moves to stand behind her husband and puts her hands kindly on his shoulders.

"Thanks, dear. I'm concerned about something with the science fair. I guess that I should tell you. Do you remember when we visited William in Nevada in the hospital? He told us that he was in there for just a small surgical procedure and he would be back to work in no time. Well, it was quickly obvious that he was not coming back to Colorado and indeed was dying. I should have been honest with his wife at that point. I should have told her about William's life here in Colorado. Now that "lie" is coming back to hurt a lot of innocent people. I should have done what was right." Mr. Menendez sits with his head in his hand, softly crying in a low, moaning tone as his upper body slightly sways.

"Listen to me. It was William's responsibility, to tell the truth to his family. He needed to be truthful; he made a choice to lie. It is not for you to defend William. Even if you did know some information, it doesn't mean that you are responsible for his life." His wife kneels down next to his side and attempts to comfort her distraught husband.

"My brain tells me that you are right. My heart tells me that I lied because I didn't let those innocent people know what I knew. It torments me." Mr. Menendez stops his swaying and wipes his red and swollen eyes.

"If you truly feel that way, dear. Take this opportunity to redeem yourself. Take the lead in this situation and help all the parties involved come to a good relationship. Talk to the mothers, sit with the girls, coordinate with the school staff, your interventions could have positive results." She wished that she could make the world better for her beloved husband; knowing all the time that she could not.

Pamela agrees to meet with Michelle at a local restaurant. It is a place that won't pressure the two women to leave if they are involved in a heated discussion. The kind of out of the way place where two women could go who need to spend some time discussing an intimate topic. Both women enter the building in a relaxed manner but greet each other with a reserved posture. This discussion may well change both their lives.

"Good afternoon, Pamela. I guess that we both know why we are here today. I also imagine that neither one of us wants to be here. However, the fact is that in some manner, our families are related. I am resolved to find the core of that relationship if you are." Michelle fidgets with the straw of her drink as she speaks to the obvious reason for their meeting.

Pamela sits directly opposite to Michelle at a circular wooden table. Her hands, which have been resting in her lap, are now massaging the muscles in the back of her neck. Her cool drink remains untouched on the table in front of her. "I appreciate the position that we are both in. I surely don't know how we got here, but I would like to know how it happened. I guess that we need to talk about our families."

"Well, I'll begin by asking you about your last name, Michelle. It is Henry?" Pamela asks with trepidation, fearing that the answer is positive. She senses that the answer to their connection lies in her answer.

"Yes, our family name is 'Henry.' Why is that such an issue for you?" Michelle stares into Pamela's eye with a look of defiance. It's as if two poker players are judging the other when the table stakes are high.

"I ask because I may know how our daughters are related. I met a man a few years ago who was working for Mr. Menendez in his insurance business. This man I know was named William Henry. He and I fell in love and formed a good relationship. He is Dacia's father. Mr. Menendez visited William in Nevada before he died and he told me of his death. However, I have not told Dacia that her father passed away." Pamela lowers her head, afraid to make eye contact with Michelle and waits for a response.

"Are you telling me that you had an affair with my dad when he was still married to my mom. If that's not bad enough, you guys have a child from that, and that child is Dacia? That's horrible. You are the woman that caused us all so much pain and trouble. You are THAT woman! Oh my god. I'm sitting here in front of you, talking to you. I can't believe it." Michelle's tone of voice is elevated so that other restaurant customers notice that both women are uncomfortable with their discussion.

"I understand that you are upset with me and the situation. You have to remember that I did not know that William was married. He told me that he was single. Mr. Menendez did not tell me anything different. Both men presented the situation as though William was a single person. I believed that I was in love with a single man. William let me believe that. William did not wear a wedding ring. He did not have any family pictures. Whenever he traveled out of town, it was for the insurance business. I didn't know that he was going to Nevada to visit his family, to see his children. Obviously, William was good at deception. I am angry and frustrated by this situation also. I wish that William were here to answer for his actions, but he isn't. We are left to deal with what he did." Pamela searches Michelle's face to detect any signs of compassion or understanding.

"You have to understand; I'm William's daughter. He was my father. Kaye is my mother. We're a family. You,

Pamela, are the other woman. Don't you understand that your relationship with my dad has destroyed our family? We trusted my dad, and now we find out that our lives together has been a lie. We can't talk to him about it because he's gone. It's horrible. Everyone is angry and sad and heart-broken. We don't care that you didn't know any of this. We don't care about you right now. We care about ourselves. Everything is still raw for us. We don't like you, but we need to deal with you." Michelle's body position is leaning into Pamela's face to the point that Pamela needs to scoot her chair back from the table so that she can avoid Michelle's seething mouth. Pamela's nose is touching Michelle's nose, and Pamela can feel the heat generating off of Michelle's flushed cheeks. Pamela backs away and repositions herself in her chair while straightening her clothes.

"Obviously, we are both upset over a situation that neither one of us created. Also, our daughters have uncovered a family connection that has linked us forever. It's also clear for me that my dad is in the center of all this. I'm angry and hurt about all of this, but I'm also mad at my dad for doing all of this. I can't talk to him about this mess, and that also makes me mad too. There seems no way to figure all of this out, and that makes me double-mad. So, all I see and feel is mad. I don't want to see or feel mad, so I need to take a deep breath and stop talking for a minute." Michelle sits back in her chair, takes a deep breath and stares out of the restaurant window as though she is looking at the most interesting thing in the entire world.

Both women sit in silence while breathing heavily. After an entirety of a few seconds, Pamela clears her throat and says, "Well, it's clear to me that I need to talk with Dacia and tell her the full story of her dad. She will have a lot of questions about William that I have been trying to avoid. I can't withhold the story now. That's got to be my priority. I guess that I don't know what to do after that. Although, I am angry at Mr. Menendez because he obviously knows the entire story of both of our families. He knew about the double life of William. If you think about it, William was lying to all of us, none of us knows the truth." Pamela's brain feels like a pinball machine where the ball keeps hitting on the side rails missing the goal posts.

Michelle takes a deep breath and adjusts her position to face Pamela. "Well, okay., we obviously aren't going to get anywhere exchanging barbs with each other. I called my mother and sister to let them know about the positive DNA tests. They are as upset as I. We also need to consider that all of this may also affect the community as well. There may be more "positive" results in this DNA testing for the science fair. If so, other families may go toward the same direction."

"I agree. I hate this situation as much as anyone. William has left us all in a real mess. He obviously wasn't a very principled man. I didn't know him as well as I thought I did." Pamela says almost as an after thought as she reflects on her life with her lover. Both women are in a high-stakes championship game where a nefarious team member has deflated the football.

"Pamela, I know that you didn't know that my dad was married, but when my mom discovered that he was having an affair with a woman living in Colorado, it crashed her world. She was a professional woman who worked for years in her field. The stress of trying to deal with my dad's betrayal was so intense that it caused her illness. The symptoms of that illness caused her to leave her career. She is not my mother anymore. I don't mean that she's gone from my life, but her joy for life is gone. She carries a burden now that she didn't have before she learned about my dad. Not only that, us kids loved our dad, and we would never believe that he could do anything wrong. When we see you, it is a raw reminder that our dad was a cheater, a liar, someone who we couldn't trust. None of us wants to remember him that way. We want to have only good memories of our dad. You took that from us. We don't like you because of that. You may be a good person, but we don't like you; Dacia may be good, but we don't like her. Now, things get mixed up. Dacia and Dove-Whispering are steadfast, good friends and probably will be for a lifetime. When Dove-Whispering learns about everyone's relationship, she will immediately know that her grandpa did something bad. She will know that grandpa hurt grandma. We don't want her to know that. It will also shatter all of the good memories that she has of her beloved "pa-pa," we don't want that either. A lot of people in our family will have a lot of pain. So, Pamela, you see even if you don't see yourself as a bad person, you are the "bad guy." I don't know how else to explain our view to you. It might be harsh, but that's the situation." Michelle sits back in her chair and is surprised to find that the scene outside has turned from sunny to twilight. The discussion with this "other woman" has engulfed her and consumed all of her sensitivities. It's as if Michelle is in the throws of a wild, tropical wave that is heading straight for the coral coastline; she sees her demise.

"I'm truly sorry for any pain to your family. We have experienced a loss also. Dacia lost a dad. I lost a partner.

Now I understand that I also lost the ability to determine if I can trust people. It is going to be a new life for me also. I don't know what else to say right now." Pamela shakes her head slowly as she fidgets with her shredded napkin avoiding Michelle's eye contact.

Both women sit quietly at the table in contrast to other patrons. The restaurant milieu has become noisy since a hungry crowd is entering for their evening meal.

"Pamela, we need to leave. I don't know if we have decided anything about all of this. I'll be calling my mom and sister about this meeting. I'm sure that you will be talking to your daughter. Mr. Menendez is somebody that we both need to talk to about this issue. What do you want to do?" Michelle impatiently waits for Pamela's response.

"I have known Mr. Menendez all of my life. At this point, I don't think that I can even trust him. Obviously, he has known all of this information from the beginning. He has held secrets for years. Trusting him will be something I will have to reconsider very carefully. He is central to both the information at school and my personal life. I still can't believe that the people I trusted have kept information from me for so many years. It is embarrassing and hurtful. Mr. Menendez has been a "father figure" for me since my parents died. I have looked to him for guidance both in a professional and personal manner. He has kept secrets from me. I can't trust him; he knows more secrets." Pamela is oblivious to the clamor of the incoming patrons and assumes robotics gestures in her speech and actions.

Both women leave the restaurant with heavy hearts. They may not like each other, but there is a better understanding between two betrayed females who loved the same man. Each one now has a duty to inform their daughter that betrayal and lies is the basis of their relationship, neither relishes the job. It is clear from the intense discussion in the restaurant that Dacia's father is also Dove-Whispering's grandfather, William Henry. Michelle and Pamela will count on their strong mother-daughter bond to help soften the trauma of the revelation. However, there is still the issue of the science fair. The decision to proceed with the program will require a combine discussion of professionals at the school level.

CHAPTER 16
ATONEMENT

*"It's when I have to acknowledge the past
and all those nameless, faceless people I'd
assassinated, that I unravel inside."*

Cheyenne McCray, The First Sin

*""You have found love in your heart and
out of small changes come great things."*

**Alan Kinross,
Longinus the Vampire: Redemption**

⋯

I t is obvious that Mr. Menendez has an imperfect love.
He tries to shelter but is not good at it. He tries to coach
people who are uncoachable. He tries to lead with honor
and dignity as an example to others who are not interested

in that form of life. He tries to be morally strong but fails on a regular basis. Mr. Menendez doesn't realize that he isn't imperfect until he looks at the destruction of other's lives. The destruction caused by William Henry is this example. Mr. Menendez tried to influence William when he saw him in the hospital on his death bed. Mr. Menendez bent down toward William, touched his cheek, spoke softly into his ear, saying "Atone, William, it's time." William was having none of it. Mr. Menendez finally realizes that he can't change others, so he decides that he will change himself, he will atone.

Mr. Menendez met Jim Sleazy when they were both young adventurers in the Colorado "boom" days. Speculating in land deals was the currency of the day. Jim was the "stepper" of the duo, and Mr. Menendez was the stalwart. There was always a deal or a fix or a flip that interested Jim. Menendez, as he called himself back then, was the "detail" man who was left to make apologies or sign contracts, make amends or repair wrongs. The two men were a powerful duo when it came to making a swift deal or a quick get-away. They didn't need to worry about tomorrow since they were already working on another keen deal.

The Denver area developed with the discovery of rich mineral earth. This discovery brought prospectors from every corner of the earth. The "sleazy" duo with its nefarious background saw this situation as a ripe garden of Eden. Their greatest heist was the development of Cheesman Park. When the cemetery got relocated Jim, and Menendez made a lot of money on that deal. They also sold a large, worthless piece of property on the outskirts of town to a young couple named "Love" who wanted to develop a hotel, knowing that the city would never develop the water rights in that area.

Well, things were going so well, they decided to hire a secretary and open an office. It wasn't a big place, just a little "hole-in-wall" so they could have an area to file papers and hide out if needed. Jim was the one who interviewed the young ladies for the secretary position. He was "boozing" in those days, so the process was getting pretty wild. Jim thought that he would try out his charms on the applicants. Menendez intervened to choose a competent girl for the position. Bernice was not only a competent secretary but made the duo into a trio. However, Jim could not mend his "Romeo" ways and soon was enticing the secretary into a romantic interlude.

Late one evening, the inevitable happened. Jim made his romantic, aggressive move on Bernice and she was defenseless in the small, confining room. It was a savage attack for which Jim never apologized. Menendez found Bernice in a disheveled condition early the next morning when he came into the office to review papers for an upcoming land deal.

Menendez went hunting for Jim with a vow of revenge. He found the guilty perpetrator at a local bar, sitting at a corner table. He was in a drunken stupor with a loaded gun placed on the table in front of him. Menendez approached cautiously. The closer Menendez got the better view he had of Jim's hand. Jim held a second gun in his hand, pressed against his heart. Menendez took another step toward Jim,

Jim pulled the trigger. The shot went straight through his heart. Jim was dead.

═══╬ ╬═══

Trepidation guide Bernice and Menendez as they review the pending cases that the unsavory team has initiated. Misappropriated funds and swindled land deals reached far into the tentacles of local society. They decided that it is time for atonement. However, quick reparation would not be forthcoming. Bernice was pregnant with Jim's baby, and she would keep the child. Long-term investment in the community was the only path to redemption for both Menendez and Bernice.

Menendez approached the young couple that bought the large piece of land on the outskirts of town. He knew that they were having trouble getting the water rights lifted for their hotel development. The couple was extremely grateful for Menendez's intervention never knowing that it was Menendez and Jim who were instrumental in the restriction in the first place. However, Menendez was looking for another reason to enamor the young couple. On behalf of Bernice, Menendez approached them to adopt her baby daughter. Bernice was a young, unmarried girl with a baby in a culture that frowned on that combination. However, there were two conditions to the agreement. One that the young couple could never reveal that Bernice's daughter, Pamela, was not their child and two, that if Pamela were to have any children, they would inherit a trust fund administered by Menendez.

Since the young couple could not have children of their own, they heartily agreed to the atonement deal. The

243

baby's name officially changes from Pamela McKim-DePue to Pamela Love, and a large trust fund, comprised of profits from questionable land deals, was legally established for the child and her legal heirs. A stipulation of the fund states that "legal heir" could be defined as broadly or stringently as the child would determine as the child reaches adulthood.

Mr. Menendez vows that he will assume a position in the community where he can watch over the child, positively impact the development of the area and assist Bernice whenever possible.

"We are meeting here today to discuss two issues. A decision about continuing with this year's science fair, and we need to decide if we want to look at the DNA results of the other "paired" students. I will remind you all that our discussions are confidential. We are professionals at this school and bound by our ethics on this matter. Some unexpected results have already occurred which will affect lives so, our oath of silence is important." Ms. Walters addresses the science fair committee at the high school a few days before the competition. The high school principal, the counselor, the Chamber of Commerce representative and the science teacher are in their final meeting before the science fair. After a discussion and vote, the committee decides to continue to with the science fair activities. The reasoning being that the school, parents, and community expect the yearly entry. Dakota Flats has entered the science fair ever since the competition initiated. The competition will continue. Ms. Walters will notify the students and the parents of the decision.

Ms. McKim-DePue and Mr. Menendez meet after the meeting. "Well, Pamela and Michelle met the other day to talk about their relationship. I talked with Pamela at length last night. They know that their daughters are related, they're related. Bernice, I talk with Pamela, both she and Michelle are very emotional about the whole DNA matching. They are angry. Not necessarily at each other but at someone who is no longer with us, William. They each cared for him and realized that he betrayed both of them. I say this in the most understanding manner, Bernice. It may be time for you to have a conversation with Pamela. It may be time for the whole truth to be known for everyone. Pamela and Dacia are loving, giving people who deserve to have a full and honest future. You can give that to them, Bernice. You need a future. I know that Pamela is going to have a talk with Dacia tonight and tell him that William is dead. Up to this point, Dacia thinks that her dad has been on a very extended trip. Pamela and Dacia have been living under the shadow of a lie. That shadow needs to be whiffed away. You can do that for them." The school counselor listens intently to her longtime friend and confidant. The secretive mood at the school in recent days has caused the student body to feel unsure. Many students have been in the principal's office complaining of headaches and vague aches and pains. The school atmosphere seems unsettled.

"Well, Michelle, how did your meeting go with Pamela?" Kaye is talking with her daughter on the phone. "I'm going to talk with Dove-Whispering this evening, mom. I'll talk with you later. I want my daughter to know the full story about her and Dacia before we talk any further. I'll call you back when we are done talking." Michelle tries to cut the conversation with her persistent short so that she can have ample time with her daughter for a conversation that will change both of their lives.

"Okay, call me right away. No matter what time it is." Kaye is persistent.

"Dove-Whispering do you have a few minutes where we can talk about something important? I need to tell you something that I found out today at school about the science fair. The results of the DNA tests came back. They indicate that your DNA matches another student in the group." Michelle pauses and waits for Dove-Whispering to understand what was just said.

"What do you mean, mom? I don't understand. How can I be related to anyone at school? I have never been in Colorado before we moved here. It's impossible. The tests probably got mixed up. That's goofy." Dove-Whispering puts down her cell phone and stares straight into her mom's eyes as if her mother is telling her a science fiction tale.

"Well, sweetie, sometimes adults do things that aren't nice that affect their children. The children can't understand that their parents do bad things since they love their parents. It's not that the parents are bad people, it's just that sometimes the people that we love do bad things. I guess that I'm having a little trouble explaining this whole thing to you, sweetie." Michelle sits on her daughter's bedside and touches her shoulder.

Dove-Whispering flinches from her mother's touch and drops her cell phone on the floor. "Who are my relatives? Some weird person from outer space." Dove-Whispering raises her voice in a sarcastic manner.

"Dacia." Michelle blurts out the name before thinking.

"What? What did you say? How can that be? She doesn't even look like me. We are different. Something is wrong." Dove-Whispering walks aimlessly around the room.

"Well, your grandpa lived with Dacia's mom when he was here in Colorado. They were in a relationship. Dacia was born from that relationship. They both loved her very much." Michelle's tone is pleading to help explain the situation so as to soften the blow for her child.

"So, Dacia is a bastard child and my "pa-pa" cheated on grandma. I don't believe that I am hearing this. Mom, it can't be true. Mom, it can't be." Dove-Whispering's voice quivers and tears fill her eyes as she collapses on her bed.

Michelle cradles her sobbing child and both slow rock as they absorb the realization of their changed world. After a few sobering minutes, Michelle breaks the silence. "Dacia's mother is also telling her tonight about the situation. I'm sure that they are also having an emotional night, sweetie. We can look at this as a good thing. It can be that we have an extended family. I know that it takes time to absorb what I just told you but the test is correct. Also, the people that knew your dad when he lived here know that the situation is true."

"Mom, I don't know what I'm supposed to do now. Everything is all messed up for me. My "pa-pa" was a bad man. I have a cousin or an aunt or whatever she is, and another family that I don't know. They have been living, and I didn't know anything about them. It's a lot of stuff." Dove-Whispering's voice trails off as though she doesn't expect an answer.

"I know, sweetie. It is confusing for me too. We will be talking to Pamela and Dacia about all of this. I guess that Mr. Menendez, the man who was your "pa-pa's" boss, also knows some of our histories. We will get some information from him too." Michelle softly cries, as she comforts her daughter.

"Mom, I talked with Dove-Whispering. It is distressing to both of us, but we will know more about the whole issue after we discuss it with Pamela and Dacia. It's late, mom. I'll call you in a day or two when I know more about everything." Michelle hangs up the phone before her mother Kaye can initiate an extended conversation.

The visitor repeatedly knocks at Pamela's door without an answer. Mr. Menendez is about to leave when the door slowly opens. "Oh, hello sir, I didn't know it was you. It was a late night for us. Dacia is upset to find out that her dad is dead. She still can't understand how she and Dove are related. It will take time for all of this information to make sense. Come on in; we can have a cup of coffee." Pamela and Mr. Menendez sit at the kitchen table and slowly sip their cups of coffee as it cools to their touch.

"William surely did stir up a nest of hornets. He is still at it even after his death. Who would have known that these two young girls would bring our two families together? I'm the other woman in this situation, but I don't want my daughter to suffer for what I did." Pamela is trying to put up a good defense even though Mr. Menendez is privy to her most intimate secrets.

"I came here today to suggest that you may want to have the two girls meet now that they know the truth about their relationships. They will see each other in school every day. The entire school body will very quickly know all the details of their situation. We need to have this whole situation out in the open before the rumors begin to circulate. Believe me; it's the best strategy." Mr. Menendez nudges Pamela into an agreement that he knows will end positively. He also knows that he is risking a full revelation of his personal history, warts and all.

"I know, sir. It is the best thing to do. It will be hard and embarrassing. It will be painful for me, but it will help Dacia in the long run. I'm willing to meet with Michelle and her family to talk about William and all that he did. Can you set up the meeting?" Pamela can't sit still while she talks about the uncertain future.

"You know that I will do whatever I can to help make this situation easier for everyone. I guess that I have as much to do with it as anyone. I could have influenced William more than I did when he was here. Maybe, I could have stopped him from all of his fooling around. I don't know. This whole thing has turned out badly. I'm more concerned about these two young girls. They are innocent. It's as though they are being tossed around in a tornado. I'll set up a meeting at the school as soon as I can." Mr. Menendez places his coffee cup in the kitchen sink without insisting on a visit with Dacia. She has encountered enough intrusions.

The Chamber of Commerce leader makes a stops at the high school before conducting any other business on this very confusing day. Upon entering the school, he meets up with the school counselor. "Well, Bernice, it's time for everyone to tell the truth. I'm arranging a meeting at the school for Michelle and Pamela. I'm sure that Dacia and Dove-Whispering will be there also. Some other family members from Dove-Whispering's family may also want to talk about things, her grandmother and aunt. I know that you and I have a long history, back to the early days of Colorado. Over the years, we have talked about atonement, we have talked about our family, we have talked about our early days together. It seems that all of those issues are coming together, at one time. After the parents and girls meet at the school, I would like to have one more meeting; if it's okay with you?" Mr. Menendez waits for his expected answer.

'Stinky-Poo' knows what he wants to hear. It's a secret held so tightly, like a clam holding onto a precious pearl. She did something many years ago that was for the benefit of everyone concerned. It was time to reveal the secret. The purpose it served has disappeared. Mr. Menendez waited for her decision. "Alright, after the meeting here at the school, you can bring them over. It's time to face the past." 'Stinky-Poo' reluctantly agrees with the community leader that the past needs its rightful place.

"Okay, then, I'll let them know that you won't be at the school meeting. I'll see you later." Both friends part company, each on a mission that will change their futures.

━◈┼ ┼◈━

The tension in the high school conference room is as high as a tightrope wire act. Divided members of the Henry family sit on opposite ends of a long conference table. Members of the science fair judges program assemble at the middle section of the table. Mr. Menendez moderates the meeting. "I don't need to say why we are all here this afternoon. The results of the science fair DNA tests indicate that both of these girls are genetically related. That indicates that their DNA has a close match. Upon learning that fact, I know a lot of discussions have occurred to determine how that situation may have happened. I will state the obvious, Wiliam Henry was unfaithful to his wife in Nevada and had an affair with a woman here in Colorado. The woman's name is Pamela Love. The affair resulted in a child whose name is Dacia Henri' Love.

William Henry is a grandfather to Dove-Whispering who recently moved with her mother to Colorado. That is when she enrolled in Dakota Flats High School. At that point, Dacia and Dove-Whispering met each other through science class and became friends. Through the science class, they decided to work on a DNA project for the science fair. That project resulted in determining that Dacia and Dove are genetically related. That knowledge is why we are all here today.

Now, there certainly more issues concerning this situation but those are the bare facts. I understand that the issues are emotional and that everyone is surprised by the information. If I could turn back time in this matter, I definitely would do that. However, I can't. So, I suggest that we go forward and try to find a positive solution. I know that I don't have a genetic issue in this, but I do accept responsibility for developing the situation in which it occurred. I do need to atone for my part in this."

The room falls quiet. All of the people are silently shaking their heads in the affirmative as though they agree with Mr. Menendez's statements; each is reluctant to speak. The ensuing conversation lasts for a few hours, sometimes loud, sometimes emotional, sometimes somber. At the end of many exhaustive hours, the extended Henry family leave the high school a cohesive unit determined to a life of making happy memories.

As Pamela and Dacia are entering their car in the school parking lot, Mr. Menendez tentatively approaches them. "I know that you two women have been through an emotional roller coaster today. However, I would like for you to look at one more issue with me. It won't take long. I will drive you somewhere just to let you see something. It will be quick." The community leader looks at Pamela with an urgency she hasn't seen him express before.

"Well, okay, if it really can't wait until later. We will go with you," Pamela agrees.

"Fine, let's take my car," Mr. Menendez says excitedly.

The drive in the dark seems exceptionally long since it is attached to anxiety. The trio eventually arrives outside an exquisite home located in a fashionable part of town. Without saying a word, Mr. Menendez turns off the engine and helps both women out of the car. He ushers them to the front door of the house and rings the doorbell. Following a short wait, the door is opened slowly by someone with a very familiar face. "Good evening, I have been expecting you. Won't you all come in?" The three tentative guests step over the threshold into the ornately furnished home. As Pamela and Dacia stare unbelievingly into the face of the school counselor 'Stinky-Poo,' Mr. Menendez speaks for the group: "Pamela, I would like you to meet your mother."